Ties

(Book 1)

Discover other titles by Michael Kelso

Novels

One on One

Identity (A One on one novel)

Endzone

Novelette

The Mall

Short stories

Dark Tales of Cryptids and Park Rangers

Dark Tales of Cryptids and Truck Drivers

Fragments of Fear

Fragments of Fear 2

Fragments of Fear 3

Fragments of Fear 4

Fragments of Fear 5

Fragments of Fear 6

The Trail

Fragments of Fear: Collection

This book would not be possible without the support of many people.

First of all, my family, who has been very supportive of my writing.

My cover designer, Chris Kudi https://www.kudi-design.com/

Emily Haynes, Sherri McCune, Sandy Beebe, and last but certainly not least, Boris Bacic. His help has been immeasurable with my last few books, as well as publishing advice in general. Not to mention being a great friend and sounding board. Please support his works as well. https://linktr.ee/Author.Boris.Bacic

There are times in your child's life you'll always remember...

The day they were born.

Their first steps.

The first time they tried to murder you...

***

One

It happened again. My wallet was missing money. As usual it wasn't a lot. Twenty bucks. Not enough to raise suspicion if I hadn't been paying attention. I sighed. How many parents have this happen all the time with children who haven't flown the nest yet? I went to my daughter's room knowing I wouldn't find the money, it was long gone, but knowing what I would find.

I went straight to her closet, slid the door open, reached up to the framework and pulled down the small box that was hidden there. I opened it and found the spoon, syringe, and lighter. I resisted the urge to throw it away or smash it and put it back up in its hiding place.

'If she's gonna do this crap, why can't she at least take responsibility to buy it with her own money?' I thought. I knew the answer was one of two reasons. Either it was just easier to steal it, especially when you have a minimum wage, part time job at the local fast food joint. Either that or the more disturbing answer, she was using more.

'This is it!' I thought. 'How long will I put up with this?'

No longer.

I heard heavy metal music blasting in her car before she got to the driveway. She parked her decade old Ford Escort and trudged up the walk. I knew right away it was an act.

"How was work?" I said as she came in the door.

"Work was work. It sucked," she said with heavy eyelids.

"We need to talk," I said.

"I'm tired," she said walking past me toward her room.

"Are you going for your stash?"

She stopped.

"What stash?" she said.

"I know all about it," I said. "I've known for a while."

She stared defiantly and I took a step forward.

"I'm going to tell you something you need to hear," I said. "You're a twisted, messed up, selfish child and if you don't change soon, I won't be able to pull you out of the hole you've dug for yourself."

Sharon squared her shoulders ready for a fight.

"Who says I want you to?" she said. "You've always said you've known what's best for me. What if what's best for me is what's worst for you?"

"How could that be? I've taken care of you, given you stability, provided for your every need."

"Really? What about my freedom?"

"You've been free your entire life. I've never held you back even though sometimes I should've."

"Free?" she scoffed. "Do you even know what it means? You've given me freedom all right. The freedom to follow your rules, to conform to your standards, to squeeze into that tiny mold in your mind of what I should be."

I stepped back and held onto the mantlepiece for balance. I glanced over at the myriad of pictures sitting there collecting dust the way I collected these memories. Birthday parties, vacations, graduation. All happy memories. Then I looked again. In every picture there I was smiling, and she... wasn't. I looked at every picture. She wasn't smiling in a single one. As if she was being held captive and told to put on a happy face. But her refusal was her rebellion.

I stared into the eyes of this angry person who had endured a lifetime of coercion.

Something within me wouldn't let me form the two simple words that needed to be said, 'You're right.' Two words, ten letters that might have saved our relationship and inevitably, my life.

"So, it's my fault that you never told me you were unhappy?" I said.

"You're my father!" she yelled. "You're supposed to know these things. Did it ever occur to you why I was always in my room?"

"I was giving you space. I gave you the freedom to be who you wanted to be."

"No, you gave you the freedom to be who you wanted to be. I know you didn't want me. I know you blamed me for mom dying during childbirth."

"That's not true," I said looking down.

"I see it in your eyes. Every time you look at her picture I see the longing, the hurt, the betrayal."

"Longing yes, hurt yes, betrayal, that's where you come in," I said. "Not because of what happened to your mother but because you're ungrateful for the sacrifice she made for you."

"A life I was forced into and never wanted?" she said. "Thanks so much."

"How dare you," I said stepping towards her. "Your mother gave everything for you."

"Like she had a choice."

"Of course she had a choice," I screamed. "And she chose you. Even if I…"

I stopped dead. The next words refused to come. The last three should've never escaped my lips.

"What do you mean? Even if you what?"

My face paled and my knees buckled under me. It was all I could do to grab the mantle causing several pictures to crash to the floor. I looked down at the shattered glass on top of shattered memories. My beautiful Amelia and me smiling on our honeymoon looking to a bright and glorious future together. On top of that was a picture of Sharon at her fourth birthday party making a mess of her piece of cake, me beside her smiling. For the first time I noticed my smiles. They were different. The honeymoon picture was sheer joy, ear to ear, nothing held back. The one at the birthday party was strained, forced. As if I was pretending to be happy.

"It's not important," I said.

"Yes it is," she said. "Tell me what you meant. Even if you what?"

"It's nothing."

"It's everything. Tell me the truth."

"The truth is your mother loved you so much she sacrificed herself for you. I'm just glad she never got to see what a selfish brat you've become."

Her eyes widened with realization.

"You wanted to save her instead of me."

"That's not true," I lied.

"And that's why you've put me through a life of hell. To get back at me for taking her from you."

"Life of hell?" I screamed. "You've had everything you've ever wanted you ungrateful bitch! I worked my fingers to the bone to provide for you. I sacrificed my happiness a thousand times over for yours and yet you never once showed the slightest bit of gratitude."

"They provide for your needs in prison too. No one ever thanks them."

"Prison? Prison? You're comparing your life to…" I screamed. And then I stopped. My face grew flush. It was as if someone had hit my pause button. I stood there, face contorted with rage, left arm hurting, taste of copper in my mouth. And then I collapsed.

***

I woke to the sound of beeping machines and the scent of disinfectant. My newly opened eyes were assaulted by white. Everywhere I looked, the walls, the ceiling, the floor, all white. It was broken up by a cabinet, a TV, and a white board that posted who would be attending to me today.

A white doctor in a white lab coat entered the room.

"How are we doing today?" the doctor said.

"I don't know how you're doing but I feel like crap," I said.

He chuckled.

"That's understandable."

"So what did you do to me?"

"Do you want the gory details?"

"Sure, why not?"

"Ok well I cut into your chest then I inserted… "

"Ok that's enough."

He grinned.

"How about the highlights?"

"Please."

"You had a couple blockages, so we did a double bypass."

"So how long am I gonna have to listen to your insufferable sense of humor?" I said with a grin.

He feigned shock.

"I'm insulted, good sir. Just for that I'll leave my wristwatch in your chest where it fell."

I laughed then stopped and clutched my chest in pain.

"Yeah, you probably want to avoid laughing for a while," he said. "Sorry about that."

"Seriously," I said trying to catch my breath. "How long?"

"If you respond well, you could be out of here in as little as a week or so."

"A week of some doc who's moonlighting as a comedian?"

He smiled.

"I promise to only do one show a night."

"That's all I can ask. Thanks, doc."

He walked out and I fell back asleep. When I woke she was there. The person who put me in this hospital bed. She was sitting in the chair beside my bed doing something on her phone. I wasn't sure if I wanted to talk to her, so I pretended to still be asleep. She stayed for hours and when she stood to leave, she leaned over and kissed my forehead.

'Could I be wrong?' I thought. 'Could it be that I've stifled her entire life? Was I blind to her needs and smothered them with my own?

Yes, she had stolen from me and done horrible things to satisfy her drug addiction. But had I driven her to it? Had my cold distance that I mistook for giving her space led her to drift even further away? Had she gone looking in other places for the unconditional love I should've given her?'

My monitor was beeping faster the more I thought about it. I needed to let these thoughts go for now and calm down before I ended up back on the operating table. I cleared my mind and slowed my breathing, then closed my eyes and drifted off to sleep.

I woke to a tingling sensation. It seemed to be coming from everywhere. I opened my eyes and there was Sharon. To my surprise she was smiling at me.

"Hello there," I rasped.

"How do you feel?" she said.

"Like a washrag that's been wrung out."

She chuckled.

"Having your chest ripped open will do that."

I laughed until it started to hurt.

"Please don't make me laugh."

"Oh, come on, how long has it been since I actually cared enough to make you laugh?"

"I'm gonna say it's been a while."

She smiled. I can't remember the last time she looked at me and smiled.

"I'm sorry about the other day," I said.

She screwed her face up into a confused look.

"You mean the other day when you called me a bitch and essentially told me you never wanted me?"

I shrank back, ashamed of what I had allowed myself to say to my daughter.

"Yes, that."

"Don't worry about it," she said kissing my forehead. "You just focus on getting better."

"Thank you," I said.

"I've got to get to work. I'll see you tomorrow."

She stepped to the door, turned back and said, "Love you."

Then she was gone.

It was the first time in forever she had told me she loved me. Lately it seemed all we did was fight. Maybe confronting her was the best thing I ever did for our relationship. I laid there and contemplated life for a while before turning on the TV and falling asleep shortly after.

I woke hours later to the tingling sensation again. I opened my eye just a sliver and saw someone pulling a needle out of my IV line. I wondered what kind of medication the nurse was giving me, but decided not to ask. Medical people usually don't like their decisions being questioned.

Sharon continued to visit me every day. It seemed like our relationship was at an all-time high. We talked and laughed and carried on. Things couldn't be better. Well, with the exception of me being in the hospital too weak to get out of bed.

One day after Sharon left for work the doctor came in and sat on the side of my bed.

"How are you feeling today?" he said.

"My mental state is wonderful, but physically I'm a bit drained."

He looked at my medical chart and frowned.

"We're a little concerned that you aren't recovering as quickly as you should."

"Really? How concerned?"

He smiled but it was strained, and it didn't go all the way to his eyes.

"Just something we want to keep an eye on," he said patting my leg and getting up. "You just rest, and we'll see what we can do to get your healing process jump started."

"Thanks, doc," I said feeling my mental state take a nose-dive.

My room was filling up with flowers and gifts from friends and well-wishers. The colorful display helped to combat the drab whiteness of the room and the scent of flowers fought valiantly against the disinfectant smell. My boss had even called to let me know my job would be waiting for me when I got better. He also broached the subject of early retirement. Having worked for the agency for over thirty years, I had a tidy nest egg laid away in my pension plan. I knew if I retired, I'd never have to worry about money again. But it wasn't just about money. It was about giving an honest day's work for an honest day's pay. My father had taught me that years ago. Did I ever pass that along to Sharon? I'm sure I did. It's just a matter if she listened and took it to heart.

The next few days felt like carbon copies of each other. Sharon would come to visit me, usually slipping in when I was asleep. She would stay for a while then sometime after she left the doctor would come in and talk to me. Asking me how I felt and saying they would continue to keep an eye on me. I wasn't feeling any better though. It was as if I was just stuck in a traffic jam. I couldn't go anywhere, just sit and wait for something to happen. The nurses came in for physical therapy, but I couldn't even breathe the way they wanted me to. I could see the concern hidden behind forced smiles and lies saying I was doing good when I knew I wasn't.

Finally, the day came when Sharon and I had to have the talk.

"I want you to know something in case I don't make it out of here," I said.

"Oh dad, quit being dramatic," she said smiling. "You're on the mend. You'll be home soon."

"I'm not so sure. But if things go bad, I want you to know you'll be taken care of."

"Nothing's going to happen."

"But just in case I want you to know I've named you the beneficiary of my estate."

She chuckled. "Your estate? You mean the same house you've lived in for the last thirty years?"

"I know it might not seem like much but there's something else. My retirement plan at work will make me a millionaire."

"Really?"

"Scrimping and saving every penny, plus some good investments really paid off."

"But that's for when you retire. That's years away."

"Unless something happens, then it's yours, along with the life insurance."

"Stop talking this way," she said tears welling in her eyes. "You're going to make it out of here because you have to. You hear me? You have to. I don't want to go on without my daddy."

She buried her face in my blanket.

"I'm sorry. I didn't mean to upset you," I said. "I just wanted you to know things would be ok. I just wanted to protect you like I've always tried to."

"I know," she said snuffling and pulling out a tissue. "You've always had my best interests at heart."

I reached up to give her a hug, but my arms felt like lead weights. I could barely wrap them around her. She hugged me back then pulled away.

"You need to get some rest young man," she said sniffling. "And I need to get to work."

"Ok. I'll do my best not to run any marathons," I said with a smile I didn't feel.

"Love you," she said on her way out the door.

I'd like to say my condition improved over the next week. But that would be a lie. I got to the point where I could barely speak. The doctor wasn't masking his concern any longer. He was stumped as to why I hadn't recovered.

I wasn't sure myself. I'd been resting. I was resting so much I started forming bed sores. My relationship with Sharon was never better. This helped my mental state, but it was the physical side that seemed to be dropping the ball.

The answer came quite unexpectedly.

I'd been having problems sleeping and was waking up at odd times. One such time I woke and was so weak that my eyes only opened a little bit at a time. I felt the tingling sensation and opened my eyes just enough to see Sharon pull a needle out of my IV line, put the cap on it, and hide it in her purse. She then sat down in the chair, made herself comfortable, and pretended to be asleep.

Two

It was hard to watch. She was drifting away in my presence and I couldn't hold on to her no matter how hard I tried.

I was so weak I could barely move anymore. The betrayal burned in me like the poison my daughter had been injecting into my IV for weeks. I had to do something.

Sharon pretended to wake up and have a pleasant conversation with me. Crocodile tears, lies, and false concern ruled her visit. She ended as always saying she loved me as she left. I now realized she never did. Even as a child she used my love to get what she wanted. Being a single parent, I wanted to help her, to be there for her. So naturally when she said she wanted something I did all I could to provide. I didn't realize until too late that I was enabling her. I was creating her later drug addiction and criminal behavior by being a 24/7 Santa Claus.

When the nurse came in I had her write down a set of specific instructions. She carried them out and two hours later my large co-worker squeezed into the chair at my bedside.

"I need to die," I told Elliott.

"You need to rest," he said.

"No, listen."

I told him all that had happened from the big fight to the heart attack to the poisoning. I laid it all out.

"Can't you call her out on it? Have her arrested?"

"If I do then she goes to jail and learns to be a better criminal," I said. "No, the only way for me to live is to die. Can you make it happen?"

He scratched the back of his neck.

"I'll see what I can do."

"I need it done today."

"Today?" he said. "I don't know if I can get a team together that quickly."

"It has to happen, or it'll be too late."

"Why today?"

"I feel like she's getting impatient and might be willing to risk giving me stronger stuff. Also, I'm so weak I'm not sure I'll last much longer."

"And what about the risk?" he said. "We don't know what she's been giving you. It could react and actually kill you."

"At this point I'm dead anyway, so it's worth it."

"I'll have to make some calls," he said getting up and heading out of the room.

"One more thing," I said.

He paused at the door.

"Make sure she doesn't get my money."

He smiled.

"Count on it."

Four hours later, three doctors walked into my room as I struggled to open an eye. The doctor closest to me gave a slight nod.

"How are we feeling tonight?" the second doctor said.

I tried to answer but had no energy. It was all I could do to notice the third doctor injecting something into my I.V. line.

"Excuse me," someone said from the doorway. "Can I help you?"

My doctor stepped into the room.

"No, we're fine, thanks," doctor two said.

He stepped in front of them. "This is my patient," my doctor said. "I don't know who you people think you are, but… "

Just then my monitors stopped their steady beeping and flatlined.

"Code blue!" the first doctor yelled. "Get me a crash cart!"

That was the last thing I heard.

***

I woke to the sounds of beeping. I opened my eyes, but instead of white, there was overwhelming darkness. In fact, aside from my bed and the heart monitor, I couldn't see anything. It was like I was laying in a bed, floating over a sea of darkness.

As I was looking around, a man emerged from the shadows. The closer he approached I began to recognize him.

"You're from the… " I rasped.

He nodded. "Yes, I was in the hospital."

"When I… "

"Coded? Yes, that was our team."

"So it worked?"

"Like a charm."

I smiled a weak smile.

"How are you feeling?"

"Safe," I said.

He smiled. "You are safe. Now you just need to focus on getting better."

He turned to leave.

"Can I ask you something?"

He stopped and turned.

"Certainly."

"How?"

"How did we pull it off?"

I nodded.

"It was relatively easy. While we distracted your doctor my associate injected a substance into your IV that made you relax so much that it looked like you weren't even breathing. At the same time we simply unplugged the wire from the monitor enough for it to look like you flatlined. We made enough of a show of trying to resuscitate you then pronounced you, slipped you out, and brought you here."

"Where's here?"

His smile slipped back onto his face.

"Someplace safe."

He turned and left.

As I recovered, I was given updates and any news I wanted.

I heard Sharon was inconsolable. That she sobbed for hours. I always said that girl would win an Oscar someday. Even when she was little, she could turn on the waterworks at the drop of a hat, or the drop of an ice cream cone.

It was amazing how fast I recovered when I wasn't constantly being fed poison intravenously. Within a week I was on my feet. In two I was walking around. By three weeks I was back to normal... almost.

Elliott stopped by from time to time and kept me in the loop on Sharon's location and her emotional state while I recuperated. I smiled when I heard she was in the fight of her life to get her hands on my money. She didn't understand why it was being held up. But she backed down when one of the lawyers said that foul play was suspected.

Once I was up and about, I started following her secretly. My boss was fine with me doing it until I'd recovered completely. He told me it was a good way to ease back into field work. I tracked her to her dealer. After she left, I paid him a visit. Soon after the police got an anonymous phone call saying a drug dealer had been killed at that location.

This continued as she had to find a new dealer. I eliminated him as well. Taking great satisfaction in destroying the people who were destroying my little girl.

Yes, I know she tried to kill me. What can I do, I'm her father.

After a few more dealers were put out of business permanently, the rest of them wanted nothing to do with her. Many of them being superstitious enough as it is, she was bad news to them. She tried making her own stuff for a brief spell. I guess watching too many episodes of Breaking Bad made her feel like going into business for herself.

That ended in a trip to the hospital. After that she had no choice but to go to rehab. She lost her job of course, but she wasn't working up to her potential anyway.

It was difficult for me not to visit her in the hospital. Not only because she's my daughter but also to see the shocked horrified look on her face when the man she thought she'd murdered walked in the door. It would've been especially fun in the early days of her hospital stay when she was still in the throes of drug addiction.

But that would go against my mission. Did I want to see her suffer? Absolutely. Did I want her to go to jail? No. Did I want her to die? The jury was still out on that one. I would've been justified in wanting it, especially after she tried to kill me and nearly succeeded. For the moment I'd have to be satisfied with watching through binoculars from the rooftop across the street. Seeing her writhe in pain was surprisingly cathartic.

Fortunately, my boss was on board with my plan. He arranged for my retirement and life insurance money to go into an untraceable fund which I was able to access. So, money wasn't an issue. I rented an apartment across the street from hers. Once she got out of the hospital, it had the perfect view of everything she did daily. My video camera, directional microphone and sniper rifle populated the three tripods aimed at her window. They were hidden behind an ingenious one-way film the agency used to prevent detection.

I sipped my cold coffee and scratched at the beard I'd grown during my recuperation. It was long and scraggly, and lord how it would itch. But I kept it as a disguise, just in case. I snickered at being both angel and devil on her shoulders. Being responsible for both her protection and pain.

I was yanked from my reverie by a knock at the door. In an instant I was on my feet, hand on the pistol in my waistband. I approached the door silently and peered through the peephole.

"Come on," Elliott said. "Open up. I know you're in there."

I slowly opened the door to let him in.

"What are you doing here?" I said.

"Boss wanted to see how you were doing," he said. "I'm in between assignments so I volunteered to check in on you."

I released the grip on my handgun and gave his hand an enthusiastic shake.

"Come on in," I said. "It's good to have some company."

The threadbare couch creaked as his massive body sat on it and he eyed my tripods.

"Can I offer you something?" I said. "Cold coffee? Stale doughnut?"

He looked around the empty apartment with peeling wallpaper and mystery stains on the carpet.

"No thanks, I'm good."

"Thanks for stopping by. I was starting to talk to myself."

"No problem. So, any change?"

"No, she went to the store around ten minutes ago. Other than that, she's been watching a lot of TV and recuperating."

"How about you?" Elliott said. "Still planning the same thing?"

"I'm not so sure anymore. I've begun to wonder if I'm partly to blame for her becoming what she has."

"You are," he said. "But in a good way."

"How do you mean?"

He leaned forward and rested his massive arms on his knees.

"You were a good father. It's not your fault she turned bad. You did all you could to take care of her needs."

"I wish I were so certain."

"You remember her sixteenth birthday party? When you bought her a car?"

"Yeah, she wanted a Mustang but I got her a Taurus."

"And she brooded for weeks. She didn't see that no kid should get a hotrod for their first car. She didn't see that you were trying to protect her. She even tried to trade it for a classmate's older mustang."

I shot him a suspicious look.

"How do you know that? I didn't even know that."

He shrugged. "Consider our line of work."

"Nope, sorry, not buying it. That wouldn't be something that would show up on the agency's radar."

He smiled and raised his hands in surrender.

"Ok, you got me. I may or may not have been keeping an eye on you at the time."

"What? Why would you surveil me?"

"I was assigned."

"For what?"

"At the time the agency wasn't one hundred percent sure of your allegiance."

"So, you were sent out to make sure I was being a good boy and following orders?" I growled.

"Pretty much."

"Did I pass?"

"Are you alive?"

"Yes."

"Then you passed."

I shook my head. "What's this world come to when you can't trust the people who've trained you to lie?"

"Go figure," Elliott said with a crooked grin.

"I still can't believe you spied on me."

"Who would you rather do it an enemy or a friend?"

"I suppose a friend."

"Then maybe you should just let it go," he said with an edge in his voice.

"Ok, what do you think I should do about Sharon?" I said changing the subject.

The couch groaned in protest as he leaned back into it.

"Not sure," he said after a moment's thought. "What's your endgame? To reform her or kill her?"

"That answer depends on her."

"Do you have a contingency plan in place for each?"

"Of course, I do."

"Then I'd say let it play out."

I sighed. "That's a lot of waiting. I'm not sure I have the patience for it."

"Then why did you start this whole thing to begin with?"

"Because she was trying to kill me and almost succeeded. Dying was my only way to stay alive."

"Irony."

"Big time."

"But what if she finds out?"

"What? That you're still alive?"

"Yes."

"The only way she's finding that out is if you get sloppy," he eyed me suspiciously. "Or if you tell her."

"Why would I do that?"

"You'd be surprised at the things you'd do for someone you love," he said with a face of stone. But there was something in his eyes. A glimmer I wasn't sure of.

"I suppose. I mean here I am at my age, staking out my daughter to protect her."

"And yourself."

"But what if she finds out and tries to kill me again?"

He looked from my eyes to the sniper rifle.

"I think you know the answer."

"I don't know if I could do it."

He laughed.

"You remember that assignment in Puerto Rico around eight years ago?"

"Yeah. I was called in to assassinate the dictator's daughter."

"Did you do the job?"

"Yeah. She was only 23. She had no idea she was being used by her father to smoke out one of our operatives."

"So you didn't want to do it?"

"Of course not. She was innocent."

"But did you?"

I sighed.

"It was one of the toughest missions I've ever had."

"That's what I'm saying. It may be tough, but you always come through. You set aside decency and morality to complete your mission."

"Yeah," I said heavily.

"That's why I asked about your endgame. You need to decide on your mission. Because once you do that, you'll follow through."

"No matter what the repercussions?"

"There's always repercussions," he said. "Sometimes it takes a while to see them."

"Speak of the devil," Elliott said motioning toward my video monitor.

Sharon was walking up to the front door of her apartment when out of nowhere a man approached her. They had words that apparently weren't making her very happy. He pulled out a gun and forced his way inside her apartment.

"Shit!" I said leaping over to my sniper rifle.

I focused the scope on her window and waited for them to enter the room. It didn't take long. He pushed her inside so hard she stumbled against the wall. She tried to escape but he grabbed her and threw her to the floor knocking over an end table full of knickknacks.

"You want me to go handle it?" Elliott said from behind me.

"Let's see what happens," I said flicking the safety off and centering the crosshairs on the man's forehead.

"You think you can steal from me?" the man's voice echoed through the speakers magnified by the microphone I had hidden in her apartment.

"I told you I don't have a job right now," she said breathlessly laying on the floor.

"Enough! No more of your excuses. Two months you haven't paid me for my shipment. Two months you've been hiding from me."

"I haven't. I was in rehab and in the hospital."

"Oh, I'm so sorry," he said. "How much more time do you need?"

"Well, I don't… "

"Shut up! You think I give a damn where you were? I just want my money."

"I don't have it."

He reached down, grabbed a handful of her hair and pulled her to her knees.

She screamed and squirmed but couldn't escape his grip.

"Well then, I guess we'll have to figure out a payment plan."

He pressed the gun to her temple and unzipped his fly. My finger tightened on the trigger.

"Please…" she said.

"Sorry," he said. "You and me are gonna have a little fun. After that? I know a guy who buys organs wholesale. I can get a pretty penny for your heart, liver, and kidneys."

"Oh my God!" she said sobbing.

"Yeah, that's right, crying makes it more fun."

My finger pulled tighter as I settled the crosshairs on the center of his skull.

As I was about to fire she swung up and hit him in the head with the antique iron she had knocked off the table. He stumbled back, stunned. She didn't wait for him to recover. She swung it again with every ounce of energy she had and hit him right in the temple.

Blood flew. His eyes rolled back in his head. He crumpled to the floor.

She stared down at him for a moment then unleashed a barrage of violence I didn't know she was capable of. She pounded his head mercilessly with the iron, bludgeoning him until all that was left of his head was a bloody puddle.

She stood slowly and looked at her handiwork.

"Wow," Elliott said behind me. "Looks like your girl can handle herself."

"Yeah," I said with a mixture of emotions as I clicked the safety back on.

Three

Sharon held it in her hand; heavy and solid, like a piece of the world and thought about all the moments that had to occur for her to end up holding an antique iron, dripping with blood from the man she just killed. The man who was supposed to save her from this madness. Instead, he dragged her deeper down the rabbit hole.

I watched on the monitor through the hidden camera. One side of me was horrified that her moral compass had been skewed so far and the other side was proud that she had been able to take care of herself.

She stared at the bloody iron for a long moment, then the expanding pool of red under the man's crushed skull. She seemed to freeze as if unsure what to do, then suddenly came to her senses, dropped the iron and ran out of the apartment. When she got to the ground floor, she put her hood up and opened the door with her sleeves. It was raining outside. Not the pleasant little drizzle of rain but the huge drops of torrential downpour that would take you from bone dry to feeling like you just got out of the pool in about five seconds.

She went up to her car and began rifling through her purse. The keys didn't magically appear on their own. She slapped her car windows in frustration as she looked back up at her apartment and cringed.

She raised her hand to hail a cab not noticing the blood running down her arm and soaking into her sweatshirt. She waved her arms in frustration as they ignored her. I pulled up in my 2012 Dodge Charger wearing a brightly colored turban. The beard and sunglasses completed the disguise. My own mother wouldn't have recognized me.

"Would you be in needing of a ride?" I said disguising my voice to sound Indian.

She eyed me cautiously then noticed the Uber sticker in my windshield. The rain washed away her caution as she opened the door and launched herself into the back seat.

"Where are we going?" I said.

"We?" she said.

"You have gotten in my car. There must be somewhere you are wanting me to take you. I am not going to give you the keys and walk away. I am going to the same place you are, and then I am being leaving after you get out."

"Sorry, I'm just a little confused right now."

"So you do not know where you want to go?"

"I'm not sure."

"Ok well while you are being deciding I will go pick up someone who is knowing where they want to go and then come back for you later."

"You're throwing me out in the rain?"

"I am not being a bus stop. Either tell me where you are wanting to go or get out so I can pick up someone else. Rain is berry berry good for profit."

"The police station."

I eyed her for a moment. I knew this was a bad move, but I couldn't tell her and keep my identity secret.

"The police station is where you are wanting to go?"

She hesitated for a long moment, then nodded.

I pressed a spot on the screen of my cell phone that started the meter.

"So why are we visiting the police?" I said pulling into traffic.

"We?"

"Again, I am driving to the same destination as you."

She sighed heavily, shaking the rain off her coat.

"Excuse me," I said as the droplets flew into the front seat. "This isn't a laundromat either."

"Sorry. I'm going to the police to report a crime."

"You know they are making these devices called phones," I said pointing to my cell attached to the dash.

"I wasn't sure if I was safe in my apartment."

"What has happened?"

She hesitated.

"It's a long story."

"In this traffic we will arrive at our destination in about fifteen minutes, perhaps longer."

"Ok, it's a long story I'd rather not tell."

"That is understandable. Pardon my asking but, aren't you technically fleeing the scene of a crime?"

"How would you know that?" she said through narrowed eyes.

"You informed me you were reporting a crime and were not feeling safe in your apartment. Those two things add up to, the crime happened in your apartment."

"You're right. I'm just so paranoid anymore," she said wiping the rain off her face with her sweater sleeve.

"It is being a dangerous world out there."

"It's not just that. Lately I feel like I'm being watched."

"Oh no, now I am being the one who is being paranoid," I said darting my eyes around.

"Ever since my father died things have gone to crap."

"My apologies for your loss."

"Why are you apologizing? You didn't have to live with him."

"Is that not the customary thing to say when someone has lost a loved one?"

"I guess. I never really thought about it."

"What sense is that being making anyway? I did not cause your loss."

"I guess it's just one of those things people say when they don't know what else to say."

"I suppose. So, you were saying how your home life was not to your liking."

"Well, he told me I was getting this big inheritance, but in the end I didn't get squat."

"Wait a moment, your father told you he was giving you a lot of money?"

"He was on his death bed."

I stopped at a red light as a fire truck roared through going the other direction.

"You would think that this rain would put out any fire."

"You'd think."

"So why did you not get the money? Did some long-lost relative arrive and claim it?"

"No, the lawyers just wouldn't give it to me. They said it was tied up legally."

"That is sounding most illegal," I said shaking my head. "They are berry berry bad for taking your money."

"I don't doubt it."

"How are you being paying bills?"

"I have a little saved up. I need to find a job though."

"You should be driving an uber like me. I love it."

"I don't think I could drive all day in traffic like this," she said. "I have a hard enough controlling my road rage just driving to work and back."

I chuckled. "I am knowing what you mean. The way some of these idiots drive it is difficult not to yank them out of their cars and beat the crap out of them."

"I couldn't do that."

"You are a better person than me."

"That's not what I mean. I'd want to, but it would violate… "

"Violate what?" I said.

"Never mind, I've said too much."

"Violate your parole?"

Silence.

"And here you are being going to the police."

"What's that supposed to mean?"

"Were you doing something to be on parole?"

"Maybe."

"Something police were not happy about?"

"Possibly."

"And here you go telling them a crime has been committed in your apartment."

"What's your point?"

I turned and looked her in the eye as we waited for the light to turn.

"Do you really think they will be believing you?"

"Of course they will, there's evidence all over my apartment. It's trashed."

"That is not what I am trying to be saying."

"Then what is it?"

"You said a crime was being committed and you were scared."

"Yeah."

"That someone was following you."

"Yeah."

"And here you are, in my car with blood on your sweatshirt."

She looked down and noticed the blood for the first time. She pulled on her sleeve trying to hide it. "Your point?"

"Am I assuming the person in your apartment is not in berry good shape right now."

She didn't say a word.

"Is he dead?"

Silence.

"Yes, that is what I was thinking."

Her eyes grew wide with panic.

"What are you gonna do?"

"Me?" I said looking in the mirror. "I am going to drive you to the police station and leave. Unless you do not pay me, then I may drag you in there myself."

She pushed back into the seat.

"Relax," I said. "I am just joking."

The tension seemed to abate, and she shot me a sheepish grin.

"I am thinking you should consider what you are going to tell them. As I said earlier, they probably will not believe you if they are already thinking you are criminal."

"It was self-defense."

I laughed.

"Ah yes, that is one that the lawyers love to tear apart."

"What do I do then?"

"It just so happens I know someone."

"Someone who can…?"

"Keep you somewhere safe until you figure things out."

"But what if I decide to go to the cops?"

"Then you go to them, that is your decision. But if you do not go right away they will believe you were fleeing the scene of a crime."

"So go to the cops right now or not at all?"

"That is the advice I am giving."

"Have you ever had to avoid the cops?"

"You might be surprised how often," I added a grin to make her unsure if I was telling the truth or not.

She sat in silence for a full ten minutes, listening to the rain pound down on the roof of the car. The wipers fought valiantly to keep the windshield dry as we approached the police station.

"What is being your decision?" I said pulling into a visitor space.

"Take me to your friend."

I nodded and backed out of the parking space then headed down the street and found a place to pull off the road.

I dialed a number on my phone and waited three rings for an answer.

"Yeah," Elliott said.

"Hello, old friend, it is me. I have someone who needs to lay low for a while."

"Is this the same someone …?"

"Yes, yes," I said quickly unsure if she could hear his side of the conversation. "Do you still have the place available?"

"Are you talking about the safe house?"

"Yes, that is the one."

"Are you nuts? You can't take her there."

"Why?"

"You know damn well why," he said almost tearing through the phone.

"I informed my passenger that a friend of mine could help her. Are you that friend?"

The phone was silent for a long moment then he let out a heavy sigh.

"Meet me there in twenty minutes," he said.

"Hey," I said before he could hang up.

"Yeah?"

"Thank you."

"Remind me what you were saying earlier about repercussions."

I smiled.

"Smartass."

I hung up the phone and headed across town.

"So your friend will help me?"

"Yes, he is being on his way now to make sure the place is good to go."

"And what is this place?"

"It is a place I used to go when I had nowhere else."

"Like a safe house?"

My eye twitched.

"Something like that."

Eighteen minutes later we pulled into the driveway of a clean little ranch house on a cull-de-sac on the outskirts of Frost Creek. Every house on this street looked exactly the same except for mild variations in color.

"Here we are," I said.

"You've got to be kidding me."

"What? Are you not liking the suburbs?"

She shot me a look.

"How can you like something you've never seen?"

"You mean your parents never showed you 'the burbs'?"

"No. I was raised in the city."

"Well, now you are here, so enjoy."

"Aren't you coming in?" she said.

"I am just a humble driver. My friend will take care of you from here."

She hesitated.

"Are you sure you trust this friend?"

"With my life," I said without hesitation.

"Thanks for everything," she said opening the door.

"That is reminding me," I said reaching into my pocket. "Here is my card. Call me anytime if you are needing a ride."

"Thanks, I will."

She walked up the neatly trimmed concrete walkway and paused at the door to wave to me. I waved back as she knocked on the door and it opened from inside.

Elliott stepped out and looked both ways then his eyes settled on me. His face was unreadable, but I didn't need to. I could hear him plain as if he'd spoken the word, 'Repercussions.'

I turned away and headed home. Thoughts rushed around in my head. 'Am I doing the right thing? Should I just let her go and fend for herself? Why am I really doing this?'

I took off the glasses and turban then scratched at my beard. I was looking forward to shaving it off. I could only take this disguise for so long.

I needed a little something to clear my head. Once I got back to Larsan, I pulled into a local mom and pop grocery store I had frequented since moving into this neighborhood. The clerk nodded at me as I stepped through the door. I nodded back and he nodded again. It seemed odd but I didn't pay it too much attention at first. I walked back the aisle, picking up a bag of chips while heading for the beer cooler. I wasn't alone. Some guy in his twenties wearing a hoodie was staring at the cooler. I glanced around and noticed another guy loitering in the candy aisle. His eyes were darting back and forth.

Suddenly the second nod made sense. The place was being robbed. I became very aware of the gun in my waistband. That was a last resort. Bad things happen when lead starts flying. People watch TV shows and think shootouts are all exciting. No one really considers the repercussions. They don't think about glass and sheetrock that don't stop bullets. They fly through them into innocent bystanders' houses, windows, and driveways.

No, gunplay is the last option. So, my decision time came. Do I walk up to the counter, pay for my stuff and leave? Or do I intervene?

Do nothing or do something?

I stepped over to the guy checking out the beer.

"Too many choices, huh?" I said to him.

"Yeah," he said.

"This one's my favorite," I said reaching in the cooler and pulling out a can of Pabst.

He nodded as I clenched my fist around the can and swung a vicious uppercut with it that broke his nose and sent blood flying. He dropped like a ton of bricks.

"Hey, buddy, you ok?" I said to the guy I'd just leveled.

His partner came running over.

"What happened?" he said.

"I dunno, he just… "

But the guy saw the blood a split second too quick. He was drawing his gun before he got to me. I saw the barrel square up with my head. I did the only thing I could do. I dropped. The gun went off and I felt something hot whizz past my ear. I shot my leg out aiming for his knee. I missed disabling him but managed to trip him. He went down hard firing wildly. I rolled toward him and buried my fist in his chest. He fired again. The gun was right next to my head. The bullet missed me by less than an inch. It hit the cooler showering me in glass and exploding several beer cans. The muzzle flash singed my hair and the sound of the shot deafened me. I knew I had one last chance before shock kicked in and made me helpless. I kicked him in the face then grabbed him by the hair and smashed his skull into the floor.

I collapsed, rolled over and laid still next to the others as beer showered down on me. The only sound I could hear was my ears ringing.

Four

I was dripping. Shaking. I could feel the joints in my finger bones rattle. The world spun around me and hummed like a swarm of bees in my brain. Nothing made sense and all I could feel was fear.

I could barely hear the store clerk yelling my name. It sounded like he was at the far end of a tunnel. I could feel him shaking me and liquid running down my face. I didn't know if it was blood or beer. The stinging sensation made me think it was a combination of both.

He grabbed me by the shirt and shook me.

"You gotta go!" he yelled.

All I could hear was the incessant, maddening ringing in my ears, but I could read his lips.

"C'mon, man, the cops are on their way!" he yelled.

He dragged me to my feet. It took me a few seconds to stand on my own. He helped me to the door, took me outside and put me in my car.

"They can't find you here, you know that," he said. "Drive up the street as far as you can go then pull over and get yourself together."

I stared blankly at his nametag that said, 'Joe'. He shook his head and ran back to the store as red and blue lights flashed off the buildings, headed this way. I had around thirty seconds until they were here. I started my car and did exactly as he told me. It wasn't very far before I pulled over and parked. I leaned back in my seat and closed my eyes.

I opened my eyes hours later to someone tapping on my window.

I looked at a young woman pointing to my windshield.

"Are you available?" she said.

I was surprised that I was able to hear her even though the ringing was still annoyingly loud.

"Excuse me?" I said.

She pointed to my windshield again. I straightened my seat and saw she was pointing at my Uber sticker.

"Sorry," I said. "I'm off duty."

She stomped off in a huff thrusting her arm in the air trying to hail a cab.

I thought about picking her up but didn't know how much of a danger I was to drive right now. I started the car and pulled out into traffic just missing being sideswiped by a delivery truck. He blew the horn and gave me a middle finger salute. I paused and took a breath to figure out where I was before I drove the remaining block to my dingy little apartment. I was never so glad to open that door and walk over that stained rug.

Once inside, I went straight to my bathroom. I was a sight. I'm surprised the girl didn't call the police. I had blood caked on the side of my face. I wasn't sure how much of it was mine, but now was a great time to find out. I stripped out of the rank blood and beer-stained clothes that had some time to ferment while I recovered. Then I took a shower, carefully scraping the glass out of my head and hair as I washed thoroughly but carefully. I dried off and checked myself in the mirror for any other injuries. Turned out most of the blood wasn't mine. I made it through with only a few scrapes on my face and a small tuft of hair that had been burned. I stared into the mirror looking at a stranger staring back at me. 'When did I get this old? Why is someone who looks like this still out there busting heads?'

The damage I feared the most was my hearing. I decided rest was the best cure. Seeing that I had no one to watch, I slept the day away. When I woke, my hearing seemed to be doing better. I dragged myself out to the miniscule kitchen and started a fresh pot of coffee then called Elliott to check on things.

"I heard you had a little excitement yesterday," he said.

"Who did you hear that from?"

"You know who."

"Yeah, tell him I'm sorry they shot up his place."

"You know it's just a cover, right?"

"I know, but it's still his place."

"So would you like to talk about your problem you dumped on my doorstep?"

"Not on the phone. How about we meet?"

"One hour at the coffee shop?"

"I'll be there."

***

Fifty-seven minutes later.

"I'm not a babysitter you know," Elliott said sipping his extra-large coffee and drawing stares from the other patrons.

You'd think they'd never seen a large man in a suit trying to squeeze into a booth before.

"I know and believe me I appreciate it," I told him. "It won't be for much longer."

"Really? And how do you know that?" he said. "Because it seems to me like she's settling in rather nicely. She's not looking for anything besides the TV remote."

"As soon as the heat's off you can send her packing."

"What heat? Didn't the cleaners take care of the body?" he said softly yet still with an edge in his voice as he looked around to be sure no one was close enough to hear him.

"Yes, but we don't know if anyone called the cops or if they've noticed she's gone."

"You're set up in your little sniper's nest across the street, have you seen any odd movements?"

"Not yet."

"It's been two days," he growled. "Don't you think someone would've made a fuss by now?"

"You're right," I sighed. "I'll go take care of the apartment today."

"Why? Isn't she moving back in?"

"How can she? The dealers know where she lives. Someone's going to come looking for the dealer she…" I looked around the crowded, noisy café and lowered my voice. "She took care of."

"Some low level low-life who was stupid enough to let her go for two months?" Elliott said. "Who's gonna care about that guy?"

"His mother?" I said with a small grin.

Elliott didn't smile back.

"Get it done," he said with a little more force than I think he intended.

"I'll have her out by the end of the week."

He nodded curtly and started the process of extricating himself from the booth while retaining his dignity. Once standing, he smoothed his tie and walked out. People parted like the red sea when he went for the door.

I sat there running scenarios through my head. How do I get her stuff out without raising suspicion? Then it hit me.

Two hours later I knocked on the super's door in Sharon's apartment building.

"Yeah, I'm coming," the super growled from behind the door.

The door swung open and the stench of old cigars, sweat, and some other pungent odor that I didn't want to identify wafted out in a nearly visible cloud that took my breath away.

"Whadda ya want?" he barked.

I expected to see this behemoth of a man and was surprised when I looked down at a man who was struggling to reach 5 feet tall. But what he lacked in height he made up for in girth. This man easily weighed 250 pounds and was built like a human bowling ball. He looked up at me staring down at him in stunned silence.

"Take a picture, it'll last longer," he said and started to close the door.

"Wait," I said. "I'm here to gather things from apartment 4C."

"Gather what things?" he said.

"Everything."

"You got some kinda warrant or work order I can see?"

"Didn't you hear?"

"Hear what?"

"She went back to jail."

"Humph, I'm not surprised. For how long this time?"

"5 to 10 is what I heard."

"I ain't gonna let you in there on just your word," he said. "She ain't even late on this month's rent yet."

"Look, man, I've got this order," I said pulling out a piece of paper and showing it to him. "It says I'm supposed to clean out this apartment and take the stuff to storage."

The super looked over the paper then shrugged.

"Alright, let's go."

I followed as he waddled up the steps leading to her apartment. I tried not to gag as the odor rolled off him in waves.

When we reached the third floor he had slowed and was wheezing.

"You alright there, buddy?" I said.

He paused at the doorway to catch his breath then nodded and handed me the keys. There must've been two dozen on the ring. I went ahead of him, picked one at random and tried it. No luck. I tried another and another. Finally, he recovered enough to climb the rest of the stairs and take the keys back from me. He picked the right one and opened the door. Five large men and I flooded into the apartment. Within an hour the place was empty.

"Holy crap," the super said. "I'm calling you guys the next time I need to evict someone."

I smiled. "Here's my card."

We pulled away with a box truck full of my daughter's belongings. A half hour later we pulled in the driveway of an empty ranch house I had bought for her on the other side of Larsan city. Two hours later the house was completely set and ready to move in to.

I called Elliott.

"Good news my friend," I said. "Your babysitting days are over. At least for now."

"It's about time," he grumbled. "Someone's been sniffing around the house."

"Do you know who?"

"No, not yet."

"I'll get her out today."

"Are you there now?"

"No."

"Alright, I'm on my way."

I hung up as I rushed to my car and headed towards the safe house. I texted her number as I put on my turban and sunglasses.

'You're in danger. Gather your personal effects and get out of the house. Start walking west, staying within view of as many people as possible. I'll be there to pick you up in ten minutes. – Your Uber driver.'

'How do I know it's really you?' she texted back.

'Check the number against the card I gave you.'

She must've listened because nine minutes later I pulled up beside her and she jumped in the car. I drove toward Larsan city in silence for a while as she brooded in the back seat.

"What's this all about?" she said after staring at her phone apparently got too boring for her.

"That house isn't safe anymore."

"Why not?"

"It just isn't."

"What about the big guy?"

"Was he there to protect you?"

"Well, no."

"Alright then."

"So now where?"

"We have another house set up for you."

"Who's we?"

"Someone more than just me."

"Give me a break. Don't talk in riddles."

"I can't tell you, so don't ask. Just know that we have your best interests at heart."

"I'm trusting you a lot considering this is only the second time we've met."

"I know it seems that way, but if I weren't trustworthy, you'd already be in prison or worse."

"Good point," she said. "But who says you can trust me?"

She shoved the barrel of a gun into the side of my neck.

"Now you're going to tell me exactly where we're going and what happened to your accent, or I'm going to redecorate the interior of your car in red, Pulp Fiction style."

"I already told you, we're going to another safe house."

"Not good enough," she said pressing the gun deeper into my neck against by carotid artery. "How long do you think before you pass out?"

I was already starting to see stars. I slammed on the brakes and whipped the wheel to the left. At the same time, I reached around and grabbed the gun as she reeled and slid to the far side of the car. I skidded to a stop in the middle of the road. I glanced out my window as the headlights of a semi truck bore down on my car. I slammed it into reverse and floored it. My tires screamed in protest, smoke rolling off them as the powerful engine proved too much for traction. A cloud of smoke surrounded the car but we had barely moved. The engine growl, the tire scream and Sharon's shriek from the back seat all merged together into one sound as I eased off the gas allowing my tires to get a grip. The car lurched out of the middle of the road as the truck luckily swerved away from us. I slammed on the brakes just before hitting a parked car. I paused to catch my breath, then unloaded the gun and tossed it back at her.

"Get out!"

"What?"

"You heard me, get the hell out of my car!"

"Why?"

"Why? After all I've done for you, and you pull a gun on me, almost kill us both, and you have the nerve to ask why? Are you really that stupid?"

I could see the rage build in her eyes.

"You son of a bitch!"

"There it is. That entitlement chip on your shoulder. Why do all of you kids have that? Have you done anything to earn the right to treat people like that?"

"Like what?"

"The fact that you don't know you've done anything wrong speaks volumes about your character."

She got out and slammed the door.

"Bastard!" she screamed as I floored it, leaving another cloud of smoke as I drove away stranding her in a bad part of town.

"Bitch!" I screamed pounding my fist on the steering wheel. "Hasn't changed one bit."

I let myself accelerate for the rest of the block then took my foot off the gas and let the adrenaline work through my system. I pulled into the nearest parking lot and found an empty space. I put the car in park, turned off the engine and tried not to throw up thinking about my very recent near-death experience.

The adrenaline crash took my energy. I wanted to go home and take a nap. But my mind wouldn't let me drift too far from Sharon.

I sighed deeply, hit my forehead against the steering wheel a few times in frustration, then started the car and turned around to go pick her up.

Five

Sheriff Ted Secrest sat in his office at his desk staring at his computer. They had these stare downs quite often Ted and his computer. The computer always won and was usually smug about it. But in the end Ted got helpful insights from such stare downs. This most recent one had yielded a pattern emerging in recent murders. There had been a string of deaths in a bad neighborhood. Nothing new there. But they were all drug dealers. Again, nothing that Ted was all that sad about. Usually such types tended to take out their own garbage.

But these were different. All professional hits with zero evidence left behind, zero. No burn mark on the floor from the shell casing. No shell casing left behind for that matter either. One in the chest, two in the head. Neat and tidy. All from the front showing at least a passing familiarity between victim and killer. Perhaps a customer or someone pretending to be a customer.

'So someone's taking out some very specific trash.' Ted thought. 'I wonder if I'm looking at a turf war brewing.'

And then there was the unmurder. That's what the lab boys had called it. A call to the police reporting a domestic disturbance and possible rape at an apartment in the same vicinity as the murders. But when the police arrived there was no sign of a body or a struggle. In fact there was no sign of anything at all. No victim, no perp, and no witnesses would say anything. It was like the entire area had been sanitized.

After the police examined the apartment where the alleged disturbance happened, they were ready to call it quits. There were lots of real crimes going on without chasing the ones that seem like they never happened. But the lab boys insisted on doing their thing anyway. They remarked about the apartment being obsessively clean. They probably would've quit too except they found high concentrations of bleach in one section of the floor and on an antique iron that was sitting on a recently repaired end table. After that they went into overdrive, tearing the apartment apart looking for a single clue. After hours of searching they didn't find anything that seemed out of place or a single drop of blood. The conclusion they came to was a professional cleaner.

A professional cleaner in the same area as a bunch of professional hits, but only this one had no body left behind for the cops to find. Why? Ted made a note of the tenant's name, Sharon Bishop. His attempts to contact her fell flat. The super had given him her cell phone number, but all his calls went straight to voice mail. It was like the woman had disappeared. Ted wondered if that was the hitman's intent. Cover a murder with a kidnapping. But what was the endgame here? Was this a new dealer moving in and taking out the competition? Who the hell was Sharon Bishop anyways. Looking her up yielded interesting results. A short stint in Larsan State Prison on drug and theft related charges. Nothing big, but an interesting piece to this particular puzzle. Another piece was there was a car outside registered to Sharon.

Ted peered inside the Ford Escort and aside from needing a good cleaning, there seemed nothing out of the ordinary. At least nothing that suggested the owner had been kidnapped.

If she was alive, was she taken or merely hiding? Was it enough to file a missing person report? Not really. Even the building super said it was common for her to disappear for days at a time. And he'd heard that she had done a hospital and rehab stay for drugs. Just another resident of a run down neighborhood in a run down part of town. A person that most didn't pay much attention to. Unfortunately for her, it seemed she may have had the attention of an assassin.

He drove back to the station feeling frustrated. It seemed like that was his general state of mind lately. He poured himself another cup of coffee and headed for his office. A few hours and another cup of coffee later, Ted leaned back in his chair and rubbed his eyes. Damn computer won the stare down again. He stretched and took a drink of his lukewarm coffee. He looked over on the wall at the large map of Larsan county which included over five hundred thousand people in Larsan city, sixty thousand in Frost creek, and just over a thousand in the strange little town of Hayalet. Add that all up and he was responsible for well over a half a million people. Yes, Larsan had their police force and Frost Creek had theirs, plus the state police did their thing and helped out when needed.

Sometimes Ted felt overwhelmed and inadequate to protect so many people. And then there were days like today. When things like this came together. Yes, all those police had their hands full with their own problems. But when Ted found something like this that had sipped through the cracks at every level, he dug in like a tick on a dog.

Sharon Bishop had become a priority. He was going to find her. And hopefully she would lead him to the assassin.

There was one other piece in this puzzle. A foiled robbery that ended in two arrests but no victim and no hero. Usually in these incidents someone either comes forward or is thrust forward as the good Samaritan. People love a story of a person fighting back against the horrible rot in the city. But no one could be found. The cashier swore he didn't see anything which proved he was lying. A beer cooler didn't just spontaneously combust and take out two armed hostiles.

It was time to visit this grocery store, but not in uniform. If the clerk was already lying to the police, another badge wouldn't make a difference.

He got up, went over to the closet and picked out an undercover outfit. Jeans, ratty old cowboy boots, and a Metallica t-shirt. He closed the blind on his office door, changed, and picked up the phone to text his wife.

'Hey, babe, gonna be home a little late.'

'Why?' came back almost immediately.

'You know, cop stuff.'

'I really wish you wouldn't.'

'It's part of the job. It shouldn't take long.'

'Whatever. Just be careful and come home as soon as you can.'

'I will.'

He sighed. He knew she hated being home alone, especially after being abducted and tortured last year. And then there was the baby. He had been deliriously happy when she told him she was pregnant. He was equally crushed when she miscarried. They both knew there were long hours involved in being sheriff. But lately, after she lost the baby, he'd been finding more reasons to work later and later.

'Is that some sort of coping mechanism or am I just trying to avoid remembering any part of that situation? That's gonna be hard to do without alienating my wife.'

"I'm going out," he told his secretary/dispatcher on his way through. "Hold my calls."

"Don't I always?" she said.

"Not that I ever remember."

She smiled. "I don't know what you're talking about."

He shook his head and left. He got into his personal car and headed toward the section of town where the murders had been happening. The further south he drove the more rundown the neighborhood became. He started to question not only why he was here but why there weren't a lot more murders happening down here. The place looked like a warzone in some spots. Burned out cars sitting on concrete blocks, buildings so dilapidated they looked like they were about to fall and take a whole row of houses with them like massive dominos. Even the streets had more potholes. Maybe the road crews didn't like spending much time down here either.

He pulled into the small grocery store and went in. The clerk eyed him as he walked through the door. Ted went back to the beer cooler, found a six pack of his favorite and took it up to the register scanning for cameras as he went.

"Evening, Joe," he said to the clerk noticing his name badge.

"Evening," Joe grunted.

"Looks like you had a little excitement here."

"Oh yeah, what's that?" Joe said without looking up.

"Your cooler back there. Looks like someone did some impromptu remodeling."

"Yeah, shit happens in this part of town."

"Everybody end up ok?"

"The punks who tried to rob the place wound up in the hospital."

"Really? Was that your handiwork?"

"Seems like I just can't remember."

"You can't remember if you shot a couple of punks?"

Joe looked him straight in the eye.

"Nope."

"Ok, do you often have robbers spontaneously combust in your store?"

"You might be surprised."

"Do you have a helper come by to take out the trash often?"

"If that's what you wanna think," Joe said giving him a hard stare.

"Is there a problem?"

"No problem at all, sheriff."

Ted picked up his beer and laid down some money.

"So you knew?"

"Yeah, I remember you from the newspaper with all that Emil Sorn and Larsan prison crap."

"Ok, then just tell me. Who took out the bad guys?"

"Don't remember."

"Why are you protecting him? Is it some comfort to know you have a killer running loose around here?"

"I have a dozen killers running loose around here. They come in every night and buy beer, just like you."

Ted turned to go.

"You know you could be charged as an accessory? I'm gonna catch him with your help or without. Your future freedom could depend on whether or not you help me."

Joe smiled.

"You have a nice day now, sheriff."

Ted walked toward the door, stopped, glanced back at the broken cooler.

"Stay safe," he said, then walked out and left.

Joe glanced at the broken cooler, then pulled a burner phone out of his pocket and dialed a number from memory.

"Yes?" the caller said after two rings.

"You might have a problem."

Six

She was gone. Just gone. I drove back through the neighborhood looking for her, but she just wasn't there. I found the tire tracks where I had nearly been a grease spot on the road and panned all around, but no Sharon.

Any other time in any other place I would've just blown it off as her hiding to try to get even with me. But not here and not now. We had made a spectacle of ourselves in a very bad neighborhood. Attracting attention like that in a place like this usually ended up in a trip to the hospital if you were lucky. Most times it was prison or the morgue, later when they found your body they made one of those TV shows about the atrocities people commit.

So, I wasn't going to get away with a quick and easy search and rescue. I was going to have to do some legwork. I took another lap or three just to be sure. Coming up empty, I went back to my apartment, did a quick wardrobe change, checked to make sure my trusty Berretta was locked and loaded, then headed out. It was only four blocks away and I had no interest in seeing my car as a skeleton, sitting on cinder blocks with all its sellable parts missing.

As I walked, I called Elliott.

"Hello?"

"I lost her," I said.

"Lost who?"

"Sharon."

"How?"

"She pulled a gun on me and almost got us both killed. So I kicked her ass out of the car."

He chuckled. "That famous temper of yours, eh?"

"Don't start. Are you gonna help me or not?" I said walking through an intersection.

"Hold on, I'll call you right back."

"Don't hang up on… "

Click

"Son of a bitch!" I yelled looking over at a large group of people emerging from a catholic church where they had just attended mass.

All eyes locked on me. Mothers glared and held their hands over their children's ears.

My face turned red as I lowered my head and kept walking. I counted the seconds until he called me back. I quit counting when I got to five minutes. In the meantime, the neighborhood was deteriorating. I knew I was getting close to where I'd kicked her out of my car. The buildings were steadily getting more rundown, and eyes were locking on me. I was on some peoples' radar.

My phone rang.

"Finally!" I said.

"Had to attend to other business," Elliott said. "Where are you?"

"I'm walking down Zahn Avenue just crossed 63rd street."

"Walking? In that neighborhood?"

"I've got to find her."

"I get that, but what good will you be to her if you're dead, or worse?"

"She was just here."

"You need to calm down," Elliott said. "You sound panicked. And you know what happens when people start making decisions based on panic."

I stopped. I caught my breath and forced myself to calm down.

"You're right," I said. "Panic never... "

The lights went out.

***

I woke in a dark room, laying face down on the floor, with my hands tied behind my back. I tried struggling but the rope was too tight. I fought my way up to a sitting position. My eyes had begun to adjust to the dark. I could see outlines of objects. There was a table and a chair. Both seemed to be made of sturdy but unremarkable material. I turned as far as I could and looked behind me. There was a wall of bare concrete block. The floor was concrete too. It seemed like there was some pattern on the floor, but it was still too dark for me to make it out.

I checked my pockets, but they were empty. No calling for help. Then I noticed someone breathing. I only heard it faintly over the ringing in my ears that still hadn't gone away.

"Hello?" I said.

The breathing became more pronounced. There was a shuffling sound coming toward me.

"Who… who are you?" I heard a woman's voice in the dark.

"I'm someone who was brought here against his will."

For the first time I smelled the faintest whiff of perfume.

"Who are you?" I said.

"It sounds like you and I fell out of the same boat," she said. "I didn't want to come here either."

"Where's here?"

"You don't know?" she said sounding surprised.

"I have no clue."

She was silent for a long moment then sighed deeply.

"You're in the lair of the Kobras."

I looked around the floor.

Apparently, she could see better than I could because she chuckled.

"No, not those kind of cobras. It's the name of the gang that brought you here."

"What do they want?"

"What everyone wants I suppose. Information, money, power."

"But I don't have any of those," I lied.

"Hmm… Then why would they bring you here?"

"That's what I'd like to know. I was just minding my own business when someone knocked me out and I woke up here."

"Do you live in this neighborhood?"

"Four blocks north of here."

"Then what were you doing here? Most decent people avoid this place."

I hesitated.

"Ah, so it's not just an accident that you're here."

"It's nothing wrong or illegal."

She chuckled.

"If it was they might help you out and split the profits."

"But it's not," I said. "I'm looking for my daughter."

She paused.

"Your daughter?"

"Yes."

"Did she get lost down here?"

"It's complicated."

I heard heavy footsteps coming down a wooden staircase.

"Pretend you're asleep," she hissed at me.

I tried to lay back down as quickly as I could, but I ended up bumping the concrete floor harder and more painfully than I wanted. I squinted one eye, trying to look like it was still closed but still seeing a sliver of what was happening. The door creaked open, and a light came on. It was all I could do to remain still and not blink from the brightness. A large man stood in the doorway. He looked at me then at the woman. I glanced over at her as well, trying not to look like I was awake. She was quite beautiful, even though she was covered in dirt and her clothes looked shabby like she had been down here for a while. I also identified the pattern on the floor I'd noticed before.

It wasn't a pattern at all. Spots of dark red splattered all around with a large spot of red in the middle of the floor surrounding the floor drain. It was dried blood.

"Wakey, wakey my little mice," the large man singsonged.

The woman pretended to still be out of it.

"That's right my pretty," he said leering down at her. "The boss wants to have a word with you."

He bent down and pulled at the front of her shirt staring down at her cleavage.

"Maybe when he's done, I get a turn," he chuckled. Then he picked her up, hoisted her onto his shoulders and carried her through the door.

She screamed, kicked, and slapped at him. But he didn't even flinch, just carried her out, then shut the door. When I heard the lock click, I sat up and looked around the now lit room, searching for anything that might help. I pulled my legs through my bound wrists so that I would have my hands in front of me, then stood and went over every inch of the room. There were no windows, only one door, the table, and the chair. That was it. The chair was preformed plastic, so it wouldn't make much of a weapon against the big guy. The table was an old wooden one that looked like it used to be used as a chopping block. The legs were sturdy and very well secured, so no help there either. I tried the door just to be sure. It was locked. I leaned against it and put my ear to the door. I could hear the faint sound of a woman screaming. My blood boiled. What could they possibly want from her? I mean aside from what any man would want from a beautiful woman, but not by force. I was raised to protect women. Except when I'm given direct orders to the contrary.

I thought about all the things I regretted doing in my life, not the least of which was killing that girl eight years ago. She was innocent and I knew it. I hid behind, 'I was just following orders.' I suppose all this crap with Sharon was my penance for such atrocities. The irony was I was doing it to keep her safe. To protect her and provide for her. That turned out well. Maybe I should've remarried. Maybe she needed a mother around. But I could never stand the thought of someone replacing Amelia. I don't know. After twenty-three years, maybe it was time to move on. Retire and go enjoy my life. Let Sharon go. She wants her independence so bad, let her have it. I thought about it for a long time.

Before I knew it I could hear footsteps on the stairs. They creaked loudly like before. That told me the big guy was coming back, maybe with her still on his shoulder. I had to take my shot. I hid behind the door and waited. At the last second, I had a thought. I grabbed the chair and set it four feet away from the door. Just enough so the door opening wouldn't knock it aside. He opened the door and sure enough he was carrying her on his shoulder. He didn't notice the chair until it was too late. He tripped over it and went sprawling to the ground. She went flying. I hesitated. Do I check to make sure she's ok? He was already getting up to his knees and that made my decision for me. I ran out through the door, turned and slammed it closed, then locked it. I had just turned the latch when the entire door shook from his massive weight hitting it. He tried the knob, but it wouldn't open so he kept slamming into it over and over. I didn't wait around to see how long the door would last. I ran up the stairs and peeked out into a kitchen. I didn't see anyone around and was about to take my first step toward freedom when I heard her piercing scream.

I hesitated. This isn't my fight. I told myself. I was brought here against my will. I don't even know that woman.

The mental wrestling match went on in my head, with self-preservation on one side and the way I was brought up to protect and defend the fairer sex on the other. It seemed like it took forever for me to decide, but in the end it was probably only a minute or so.

I slumped my shoulders. I knew I wouldn't leave her behind. I rummaged through a drawer and found steak knives. I used one to free my hands, then I went back down to the basement, weapon in hand. As I snuck down the stairs I tried to be careful and go slow so they wouldn't make any noise. I made it to the last one before the wood made the most ungodly loud creak. It was worse than you'd hear in a cheap 'B' horror movie. I cringed, hoping he hadn't heard and I would still have the element of surprise on my side.

She wasn't screaming, but I heard him say, "Now it's my turn."

I knew that couldn't be good. My imagination took me to where he was thinking and my blood started to boil again. Do I let another innocent pay for my misdeeds? Do I let another woman die so I can carry on with my life? If I leave, I'm just as guilty as the big guy for whatever happens to her.

This was it. Fight or flight?

I snuck up and as quietly as possible unlocked the latch. I turned the knob when suddenly the door was flung open. Having a grip on the knob threw me off balance and I tumbled into the room. A massive fist met my face as I looked up to get my bearings. He hit me so hard my skull bounced off the concrete and the lights went out again.

Seven

"Ouch!" Ted said. "That had to hurt."

The man laying in the hospital bed didn't say anything. He refused to look at Ted.

Ted, for his part looked the man up and down.

"Broken jaw, concussion, facial lacerations," Ted said. "Damn, man, I'd be pissed at the guy who did that to me,"

The man tried to roll away from Ted, but the leg shackles secured to the bed frame got tangled and wouldn't let him.

"So, you're just gonna play the strong silent type?"

Ted looked at the machines that monitored the man's vital signs. He stepped to the end of the bed and picked up the clipboard with his chart on it.

"But hey, on the bright side, it looks like you're on the mend, Jose'," Ted said reading the name off the chart. "Pretty soon you'll be healthy enough to go to prison."

Jose's eyes widened.

"I'm sure they'll have a nice soft bunk for you like this hospital bed. And I'm sure they'll go out of their way to give you special food. They'll just take whatever you're having for that meal and throw it all in a blender so you can drink it through a straw. That should taste amazing don't you think? And I'm sure none of the kitchen workers will be upset about having to cook special meals for you. And there's no way they would add any 'special sauce' to your mealshake."

Jose' narrowed his eyes at Ted. Shooting him a look that was somewhere between fear and loathing.

"Maybe if you're lucky they'll give you Emil Sorn's old cell," Ted said with a smile.

Jose' held up his hand with the oxygen sensor on it and gave Ted the finger.

Ted chuckled. "I guess that means you don't want to answer any questions."

Jose' held up his other hand as far as he could with the handcuffs attached to the bedrail and gave Ted the finger with that hand.

"That's ok, I didn't need your testimony anyway. I already got everything I need from your buddy. I was just looking for a confirmation."

Jose' rolled toward Ted with a questioning look.

"What, you didn't know? Your partner's getting released. He's all better, just a few scratches. He's not going to prison like you. See, he rolled on you. Said the whole thing was your plan. And seeing how you can't really testify in your condition… "

Jose' held up his hand and made a writing motion.

Ted handed him his small notepad and a pen.

Jose' wrote, 'Bullshit!'

Ted smiled.

"I'll be right back."

Five minutes later he rolled the other thief into the room in a wheelchair.

"I thought we might have a nice little chat," Ted said to the man in the wheelchair. "You see, Chuck, your buddy Jose' here rolled on you."

"What?" Chuck said coming out of his wheelchair but then being yanked back down by the leg irons attached to his ankles.

"I told him that you said you had nothing to do with robbing that store and that you said he was the mastermind. Here's what he wrote."

Ted held up the note that scrawled, 'Bullshit!'

"What the hell?" Chuck yelled at Jose'. "You came to me and said how easy this was gonna be. You set me up you piece of shit!"

Chuck tried to wheel his chair closer to the bed swinging his arms clumsily trying to get at Jose' who was leaning over the side of the bed swinging back in the most laughable attempt at a fight Ted had ever seen. He was almost tempted to let it happen and take video of it. Hell, he might even get featured on one of those funny video shows. Then his better judgement intervened and Ted got in Chuck's way, pushed him back in the corner, and locked the wheels.

"Now if you boys can't be civil with each other I'm afraid I'm gonna have to end this little visit, as pleasant as it's been," Ted said.

Chuck was glaring at Jose' who was glaring right back.

"Ok, here's what I'm gonna do," Ted said. "I need something to go on. If you two can give me something that leads to this other guy I might be able to get you time served."

"What other guy?" Chuck said.

"The one who put you two in the hospital," Ted said.

"Oh, him," Chuck said. "I'd love to give you his head on a platter, but I just don't know anything. He came out of nowhere, beat the crap out of us and disappeared."

"You don't have anything?" Ted said. "Can you give me a description, the clothes he wore, how he talked, anything?"

"I wasn't focused on him at the time," Chuck said.

Jose' started banging on his bedrail. Ted looked over and he made the writing motion. Ted handed him the pad and pen.

He wrote, 'Clerk knew him.'

Ted showed it to Chuck.

"Oh yeah, I did hear the clerk yelling at him."

"What did he yell?" Ted said.

"He told him the cops were coming and then he said something like, 'You can't be here.'"

Jose' banged the bed again. Ted took the pad over.

He wrote, 'You know you can't be here.'

Ted read the note then showed it to Chuck.

"Yeah, that's what he said, 'You know you can't be here, or they can't find you here."

Ted narrowed his eyes and thought about the cashier, Joe.

"Thank you, boys," Ted said. "You've been very helpful and I'll talk to the judge on your behalf. In the meantime, hope you feel better."

Ted headed out the door then stopped.

"And try not to rob any more stores, it doesn't end well," he said. "You two are lucky you didn't get your heads blown off."

Chuck looked at Jose' and their faces both paled.

Ted headed out to his car. It was time to pay close attention to Joe the clerk.

Eight

I opened one eye. I tried to open two but my left eye refused to cooperate. It let me know it was still there though. It was pounding like the drums in a Thanksgiving day parade. I looked around. This time the lights were on. I was tied to the chair tightly by my hands, feet, legs, and arms. I guess he didn't want a replay of my escape attempt. She was sitting in the corner, leaning against the wall, staring at me.

"I'm sorry," I said.

"What?"

"I'm sorry," I said a little louder.

"I heard what you said, I'm just unsure why you said it."

"It's the polite thing to say when you do something wrong?"

"What did you do wrong?"

"I shouldn't have tried to escape. I should've rescued you. I should've planned better to help you get out when I came back."

"Why did you come back?"

I mumbled.

"What?"

I looked away and mumbled.

"What are you saying?"

I sighed.

"I came back for you, ok?"

"Why would you do that?"

"Because I didn't want him to hurt you anymore."

She looked at me with an expression I wasn't sure of. It almost seemed like awe.

"What makes you think I'm worth saving?"

"Isn't everyone worth saving?" I said. "Besides…
"

"Besides what?"

I looked away.

"No, you don't get to do that," she said getting up and walking over to stand in front of me. She held my chin and pulled it gently up so I was looking her in the eye. Her eyes reminded me of Amelia's.

"Besides what?" she said quietly.

I didn't say anything for a long moment, as I thought of my wonderful wife Amelia I had lost so long ago. She waited patiently until I gave in.

"Besides, you're too beautiful to be left to a brute like that."

She looked at me with a new twinkle in her eye. She leaned down and gave me a very gentle kiss on the lips. When I opened my eye, she was smiling at me. She turned around, tucked her hair behind her ear, and went back to leaning against the wall.

"You're pretty stupid," she said. "You know that?"

"Yeah, I know."

"You're gonna get hurt or killed for some T and A?"

"Is that all you see yourself as?" I said. "Because I see a lot more."

She turned her head but I could still see her blushing.

"So how are we gonna get outta here now?"

"Did he search me after he played basketball with my skull?" I said.

"I don't think so."

"Well then you could come over here and help me out."

She came over and knelt right in front of me.

"What would you like me to do?"

My mind flooded with things I would like her to do, but none of them were appropriate at the moment.

"In my right shoe there should be a knife."

She pulled my shoe off and sure enough there was a second steak knife hidden there.

"Now what?" she said, still kneeling in front of me.

I had to force my mind to focus on escape.

"I think cutting my ropes would be a good start."

She smiled and leaned over to cut my legs free. I made myself look at the ceiling, the wall, anything but her clearly visible cleavage as she finished cutting. She cut the ropes to my legs, then my arms and hands. Still kneeling between my legs, she said, "There you go. You're free."

I was shaking. I wanted her so bad, but I forced myself to get up and stretch. I turned away knowing I had a hard on but pretending to need more time to stretch. All the while I was thinking of kittens and baseball to try to get back to normal. When I turned back toward her, she wore a mischievous little grin.

"So now what?" she said with her hands on her hips.

"Well, unless we can saw out of here with a steak knife, I guess we wait."

"And what do we do while we're waiting?" she said leaning seductively against the wall and tapping the flat side of the knife against her palm.

"We plan how to get out," I said making sure to focus on her eyes when I spoke to her.

"How long do you think that will take?" she said running her fingers up and down the knife blade.

I made myself focus on escape.

"Until he comes back," I said. "How long was I out?"

"Probably an hour or two."

"Probably?"

"There aren't any clocks down here," she said, showing me her wrists. "And I'm not wearing a watch."

For the first time I noticed her fingers. Not only was there no wedding band. There was no impression of one either.

'Focus on escape. Focus on escape.'

"So, what were you doing down here?" she said.

"In the basement?"

"You know what I mean, smartass. What were you doing in this part of town?"

"Can't a guy take a leisurely stroll without getting dragged into a basement Pulp fiction style?"

She glared at me, unamused.

"I already told you why I'm here. I was looking for my daughter."

"What was she doing int this part of town?"

"Looking for the Mona Lisa, how should I know? All I knew was she was in trouble."

"And how did you know that?"

I froze. I started to open my mouth, then closed it. She had me.

"Yes?" she said waiting for the answer.

"I may or may not have, accidentally… " my voice trailed off.

"Go on."

"Left her here."

She straightened and shot me a glare.

"How old is this daughter?"

"Twenty-three."

"And you left her on the streets? These streets? And now you're back looking for her like what, some hero?"

"It's more complicated than that."

"Uncomplicate it for me," she said folding her arms across her chest.

"She pulled a gun on me."

"And why would she do that to her own father?"

"Well, she may not technically know I'm her father."

"What the hell are you talking about?"

"She thinks I'm dead."

"And why would she think that?"

"Because she tried to kill me."

"Why?"

"Because she's a selfish bitch."

She stared at me incredulously.

"Back up to the part where this starts making sense."

"My wife passed away giving birth to her. I raised her as a single parent. Apparently, I didn't do a good enough job because she resented me and ended up being an entitled brat who got addicted to heroin. When I confronted her about it, we got into an argument which ended in me having a heart attack."

"And that's why you say she tried to kill you?"

"No. When I was in the hospital, I caught her repeatedly injecting drugs into my IV line. The doctors couldn't figure out why I wasn't getting better. It was because she was poisoning me slowly."

"But you confronted her, and she stopped, right?"

"No, I went another route."

"Which is… ?"

"Faking my own death."

Her mouth fell open.

"Are you serious right now?"

"Yes. A friend helped me do it."

"Must be some connected friend."

I didn't say anything.

"So, what happened after you died?" she said.

"I kept an eye on her. Protected her."

"After she tried to kill you?"

I shrugged. "She's my daughter. The only family I have."

"Ok, I get the whole 'family is family' thing. Why did you go from protecting her to abandoning her in the worst part of town?"

"She pulled a gun on me."

"Is this bitch crazy?"

"Well, she was under some stress. She had difficulties with one of her former dealers and she had to find somewhere to hide."

"Translation, you killed her dealer and she had to run."

"Yes and no," I said. "I may or may not have killed some of her dealers to keep her safe, but she killed this one and I helped her hide in a safe house."

"How did you help her without her knowing it was you?"

"I disguised myself as an Uber driver who knew a guy."

"And she fell for that?"

"When there's a dead man laying in your apartment you might be surprised what you believe."

"Really?" she said.

"So once the safe house became compromised, I took her to a new one. On the way she pulled a gun on me."

"Why?"

"Because she's an entitled bitch."

She narrowed her eyes at me.

"And that's the only reason?"

"She kept asking where we were going and I told her somewhere safe."

"And you expected her to just trust you?"

"Why not? I was the one who was protecting her. I found the safe house for her. Why wouldn't she trust me?"

"Maybe she thought it was all an elaborate ruse."

"Why would she think that?"

She put her hands on her hips.

"This from the man who faked his own death only to hide his identity in the name of protecting her?"

"Alright, I see where you're going. Maybe she felt justified."

"And… ?"

"Maybe I overreacted. But she nearly killed us both when she pulled the gun while I was driving and sent us into the path of a truck."

"Did she know that was going to happen?"

"I don't know."

"So you what, kicked her out of the car?"

"Yes," I said lowering my head. "I screwed up and now here I am a hostage for God knows why and I still don't know where she is."

"Maybe she doesn't want you to know."

"But I'm her father."

"She doesn't know that. To her you're just some guy. An Uber driver that helped her out once."

I opened my mouth to refute it, but she was right. Sharon didn't know me, at least not this me. Her father was dead, she was struggling with rehab, dealers coming after her, and now this guy who helped her was taking her away from a safe place to somewhere she didn't know.

The stairs creaked.

"Shit!" I said. "He's coming. Give me the knife!"

"I've got it. You hide behind the door and grab him, then I'll come up behind him with the knife."

"What? No! Give me the knife."

I could hear the last step creak. I knew he was almost at the door.

"Get behind the door," she hissed.

I had no choice. I darted behind the door. I waited as the lock clicked and the door opened. As soon as he stepped in the door, he saw the empty chair.

"Where is he?" he said to her.

She glanced over at me, giving away my position.

'What the hell?!?' I thought. 'She threw me under the bus.'

He turned and started toward me. I got into my best defensive stance, knowing this was gonna be the fight of my life. He took two steps and stopped, then raised his hands.

'What?'

I noticed the knife against his throat.

"Take us to your boss," she said.

"I can't do that," he said glaring at me.

"Do it, or the next stain on this floor will be your blood."

"If that's what you gotta do," he said. "But before you do, you should know that I was sent here to bring you both to the boss."

"Then let's go," she said.

"No."

"Why not?"

"I'm not gonna let you show up holding a knife."

"Too bad. Not your choice," she said pressing the knife into his throat.

"You don't honestly think I'm the boss's only guard, do you?"

She hesitated.

"Give me the knife and we all go see the boss or kill me and we all die. Your choice."

His hand shot up with a quickness I didn't think he possessed. He grabbed her hand and wrenched the knife out of it. He turned on her with menace in his eyes.

She glared right back at him.

"Well, are you gonna take us to your boss or not?" she said.

He squared up like he wanted to take a swing at her. I could see the conflict in his eyes between what he wanted and what the boss wanted.

He huffed, shot a look at me, then said, "Let's go."

Nine

We followed the giant of a man out of the room and up the stairs. When we got to the top and walked through the door he had opened, we realized what a mistake escape would've been. Five armed men, each nearly as big as the one we were following stood waiting for us in the room. They followed in line behind us as our guide continued walking, heading up a second set of stairs. The place looked like a well-kept apartment.

We followed along, heading up another set of stairs. Our guide barely fit between the walls as we marched. It ended in a short hallway with a door on each side of the wall and one at the end. We continued to the last door. He opened it and stepped inside. He stepped to the side allowing us into the room followed by the rest of the bodyguards. The room was empty except for a small, raised platform at the far end of the room with a large chair on it that resembled a throne. The walls were painted deep crimson and the carpet looked like crushed velvet. There were candelabras along the walls with lit candles in them. The throne was covered in the same velvet as the floor. I noticed in the corner there was a large roll of plastic sheeting. And there was a faint smell of bleach in the air. All in all, this room did not give me a good feeling.

We all stood and stared at the empty seat.

"Well," I said. "Where is he?"

My cellmate smiled and walked past me, stepped up onto the platform and sat in the chair. The bodyguards made no move to stop her. In fact, if anything they stood a little straighter, almost like they were standing at attention.

"You've gotta be kidding me," I said.

She smiled, but it wasn't a friendly one.

"What, a woman can't be a ruthless crime boss?"

"It's just not what I expected. But why the ruse? Why put on the act?"

She shrugged.

"Easiest way to get to the truth."

I nodded.

"So did you get what you wanted?" I said.

"Was there anything else you were hiding?"

"Always."

She cocked her head.

"Anything I need to know?"

"Not really."

She looked past me to her bodyguards and twitched her head to the side.

In a heartbeat six glocks were pointed at my head.

"Don't you have secrets?" I said.

"Of course I do."

"Exactly. We all have secrets. That doesn't mean I lied to you about anything. I'm here looking for my daughter."

She pondered for a long moment then looked down for an instant. The glocks disappeared.

"Does that mean you'll help me?"

She sighed.

"I've already put feelers out in the neighborhood. I haven't heard back that anyone has grabbed a woman off the street in the last day or two."

"Has anyone seen her?"

"What does she look like?"

"Do you have my phone?"

She nodded to the big guy who reached into his pocket and pulled out my phone. He handed it to me and I looked through the pictures until I came across one of her. I gave the phone to her.

"I've seen this girl," she said. "Two days ago."

"Where?"

"She got out of a black Charger that sped away."

I tried to keep my face impassive.

"What happened then?"

She paced on the street while talking on her phone very animated. A few minutes later a car stopped, she got in and left.

"Did you happen to get the license plate?"

"Regrettably, I did not. At the time it didn't seem like something I would need. Some internal squabble that was settled without my intervention."

"How often do you intervene in such squabbles?"

She grinned.

"More often than you might think."

"So I went through all this for nothing?"

She looked at me and her face softened just a bit.

"Why did you really come back to rescue me?"

"Exactly why I told you."

She looked at my phone then typed in her number.

"If you ever need anything, just give me a call."

She handed my phone back.

"You too," I said. "Maybe you should get my number."

She grinned. "I already did."

"So am I free to go?"

She nodded.

I turned to leave, and the guards parted ways for me. I stopped at the door and turned back.

"Why did you grab me?"

She shrugged.

"You were cute, and I was bored."

My heart raced. I had to force myself not to smile.

"Is this the way you usually introduce yourself to cute men?"

"I don't get invited to many social gatherings."

"Fair enough," I said. "Perhaps I could take you to one someday."

Her face lit up then she quickly hid it with a mask of impassiveness.

"Perhaps," she said.

I turned to leave then stopped.

"I didn't get your name," I said.

"No, you didn't," she said with a sly grin.

I gave her a 'really?' look, then dropped to one knee.

"Forsooth, milady, I pray might you honor me with the knowledge of thou name?" I said looking up at her.

She put her hand up to her mouth to hide her smile and one of the big guys chuckled softly.

She composed herself, uncovered her mouth and said, "Eva."

I nodded, got up and walked through the door unmolested. It wasn't until I was walking down the steps that I finally allowed myself an ear-to-ear grin.

I was met at the door by another large bodyguard who handed me my gun and clip in two different hands. I stuck each in a separate pocket.

I stepped outside and was surprised to find it was night. The cool air felt good on my swollen eye. I reached up and touched it. Yep, it was still tender. I started walking towards my apartment.

As I made my way home, I started thinking about Sharon. Was it time to come clean and let her know I was still alive? To let her know that I knew she'd tried to kill me, and I wasn't going to return the favor? I had already protected her several times over, what more proof would she need?

As I was engaged in my thoughts, I passed a streetlight that had a man leaning against it. He didn't stand out in any way. He had on clothes that bordered on shabby but not enough to look like he was homeless. He was staring at his phone, trying to look like he was bored but his eyes were alert and took in his surroundings every few seconds. He caught my eye and gave me a subtle nod.

I returned it as I looked across the street at another streetlight that had a similar looking man leaning against it. He also nodded. As I continued the next light had a young lady leaning against it. She was dressed similarly to the men only a little more revealing, but not enough to be a lady of the night. She also nodded.

This continued until I was one block away from my apartment. I wondered to myself at the size of Eva's network as I stepped into a local mom and pop grocery store. I roamed the aisles looking for some supper. I didn't remember the last time I had eaten. I grabbed some sandwich steaks, a pack of burger rolls, a steak, and a beer. One of the sections of the beer cooler was covered by a sheet of plywood. I glanced left and right to make sure I wasn't going to have a replay of the last time I pulled a beer from a cooler.

It didn't appear that the store was being robbed so I took my items up to the register. Joe looked at me with no discernable reaction. He rung up my items and scanned the aisles to see if anyone was in earshot.

"Rough night?" he said.

"Not as bad as last time," I said. "I don't think I ever told you thank for your help."

"You should get that eye looked at," he said as he rang up the items.

"Got it covered," I said pointing at the steak.

He shook his head.

"Maybe next time you should avoid that neighborhood."

"But I met some interesting people," I said.

"Stay away from her," he said. "She's trouble."

"What are you, my babysitter now?"

"You know I am," he said telling me the total.

I handed him two one hundred dollar bills.

"Keep the change."

"Thanks, mister," he said as a lady stepped up in line behind me.

"Have a nice day," I said walking toward the door.

"You too," he said. "Stay safe."

I thought about what he said as I walked the rest of the way to my apartment. Of course, Eva was trouble, but was she more trouble than I could handle?

I made it the rest of the way to my apartment without incident. I stepped in, turned on the lights, half expecting someone to grab me.

'That's the way my life has been going lately.' I thought.

I started cooking the sandwich steaks, opened the steak, grabbed a beer, and went to my old worn-out sofa.

I plopped down, took a long swig of beer, then leaned my head back on the pillow and put the steak on my eye.

I woke to a high piercing beeping sound. I jumped up and looked around at my smoke-filled apartment. I followed the sound to the kitchen and took the skillet with the incinerated sandwich steak off the burner then turned the unit off. I grabbed the smoke detector and ripped the battery out of it.

After taking a sigh of relief, I turned my ceiling fan on and opened my windows. I came back to the kitchen and scraped out the skeletal remains of my sandwich steak then washed the pan and started cooking another one. I had just gotten the sandwich made and was about to take a bite when there was a knock at my door. I sighed, set the sandwich down, and went to see who it was. The blue uniform I saw through the peephole didn't comfort me. I unlatched and opened the door.

"Can I help you, officer… ?" I said.

"Morgan. Yeah, we got a noise complaint," the mid-forties man said with a patch on his shoulder that said Larsan Police. He glanced around me into my apartment.

"Sorry about that, Officer Morgan," I said. "It was my smoke alarm. I fell asleep and accidentally left my stove on."

"Anything else going on?" he said craning his neck to get a better look.

I blocked the door as best I could, realizing what was really happening. I had opened the window to let the smoke out and forgot my sniper rifle was sitting on a tripod right in front of it. Without the one-way mirror of the glass, any neighbor across the street could easily see it. Nosy neighbors aside, I'm sure it wasn't very comforting to see a high-powered rifle aimed in the general direction of their home.

"Nope, nothing happening here. Just took a nap."

"That's quite a shiner you got there. How'd that happen?"

"Resisting arrest," I said smiling.

He didn't think my joke was funny. In retrospect it probably wasn't the best thing I could've said, but hunger, fatigue, and sleep deprivation is a bad combination. It can do terrible things to your judgement.

"Alright smartass, let me in that apartment."

I blocked his way. He outweighed me by a good fifty pounds or so, but most of that was belly.

"Do you have a warrant?"

"No, I don't, but since you told me there was a smoke alarm, I have to inspect the apartment to make sure there is no threat to the rest of the building."

"That's not a real thing."

"Are you resisting an officer?"

"Yes, but I'm not resisting arrest."

"So, you're ok with me arresting you?"

"That's not what I said and no, I'm not ok with you arresting me."

"Then you're resisting arrest."

"No!"

"Is that a concealed weapon I see in your pocket?"

I looked down, remembering the pistol I hadn't put away yet.

"I have a permit for that."

"I'd like to see it."

"I'll go get it."

I tried to push the door closed but he had wedged himself in to where that was impossible.

"Are you assaulting an officer?"

"No, if you move and let me close the door, I'll go get my permit."

"I can't do that."

"Why not?"

"I have suspicion that a crime is being committed in this apartment."

"Ok, you win."

"You're gonna let me in?"

"No, I'm gonna resist arrest."

Ten

Of all the rotten luck this guy has to work evening shift. Ted thought sitting in his car watching the small local grocery store instead of where he'd rather be, at home with his wife. He knew she hated him staying out late. He knew she hated him being on stakeouts. He knew that she hated him being a sheriff ever since she'd been kidnapped.

He knew a lot of things he should've changed to help his marriage, but he didn't. He wanted to be the best husband he could be, but sometimes that got in the way of the job. And the job had to take precedence sometimes, especially when there was a serial killer on the loose. Sure, the guy was killing scumbag drug dealers, but who knew when that would change. And besides, killing anyone was still against the law last time he checked.

Ted's focus was broken when he saw the back door open, and the clerk named Joe step out with two bags of garbage. He threw them in the dumpster then pulled out a pack of cigarettes and lit up. As he stood there smoking Ted thought he saw Joe moving his mouth as if he was talking to someone. The back of the store was not well lit. Above the door was a yellow bulb that was struggling against the dark as best it could, but seemed like it was fighting a losing battle.

There were shadows everywhere behind the store. Anyone could've snuck around behind the dumpster while Ted wasn't paying attention. The seemingly one-sided conversation continued until Joe's cigarette was gone. He threw the butt on the ground and stomped it out, then went back inside.

Ted made a note to bring a pair of night vision binoculars for tomorrow's stakeout. He was sure there was a pair somewhere in the armory, if no one had borrowed them without telling him, which wouldn't be the first time.

His thoughts were interrupted when Joe walked out the front door and headed for the parking lot. Ted paid close attention to which car he got into. He tried to get a picture of the license plate with his point and shoot digital camera. He wished he had the budget to buy one of those fancy cameras with the giant lens that look like they could take pictures of mars, but he burned up his technology budget for the year on the night vision binoculars.

He zoomed in as close as he could and took two pictures before the screen flashed, 'memory card full'.

"What?" Ted said. "It can't be full. What's on here anyway?"

He pulled up the menu and started going back through the pictures. After two blurry shots of the license plate, he came to a selfie of him and Alice at the beach on their honeymoon. He kept flipping through finding more and more honeymoon pictures, including the videos he took of the honeymoon night.

"I'll have to save those to the computer before tomorrow night too," he said.

He looked up and Joe's car was gone.

"Dammit! I was too busy looking at pictures and lost him," Ted said. "I guess I'd better go home and see the missus."

Ted pulled in the driveway after midnight. He opened the door as quietly as possible and locked it behind him. He pulled off his boots and left them at the front door. He crept to the bedroom trying to avoid that one creaky spot in the floor and crawled into bed. She was sleeping so Ted tried not to wake her. He settled in and carefully laid his arm over her. As soon as he touched her she sat bolt upright.

"Who is it?" she said frantically.

"It's just me, baby," Ted said.

She calmed her breathing then laid back down.

"How was your evening?" he said.

"Lonely," she said.

"Sorry. Once I catch this guy, I'll be home at a decent hour, I promise."

"Until the next guy comes along, and the next, and the next... "

"What are you saying?"

"Never mind, Ted, just go to sleep."

"No, I wanna know what you mean."

"Nothing, Ted, I don't mean anything. I'm just tired and want to go to sleep."

Ted stared at the back of her head for a long moment.

"Goodnight," he said.

The answer he got back was a soft snore.

'I've gotta catch this guy so I can save my marriage,' he thought.

Alice lay there, eyes open, pretending to snore, tears streaming down her face into the sheet.

Eleven

"No, I'm gonna resist arrest," I said to the officer standing halfway in my doorway.

"What?"

I tried to shove him out into the hall, but he turned with surprising speed leaving me flailing at air and him in my apartment. I quickly got up and rushed back inside to find him staring in awe at my three tripods. One with a camera mounted on it, one with a directional microphone, and the last with a sniper rifle.

He turned towards me with an evil grin on his fat face and pulled out his pistol.

"You're under… " that's as far as he got before I launched my shoulder into his massive belly.

He landed hard, knocking the wind out of him. I ran to my bedroom, grabbed my go bag and dashed out the door.

"Stop!" was all I heard as I flew down the stairs. At the entrance I was greeted by flashing red and blue lights. I paused, not knowing if he had a partner or not. When no one said anything, I went around to the driver's side of the car, pulled out the keys and threw them as far as I could. Then I locked the car's doors and slammed it shut. He stumbled through the door and watched in horror as I threw the keys and locked him out of his own car.

He recovered enough to fire a few potshots at me as I dove into my Charger and sped away.

I pulled out my phone and dialed a number.

"That was pretty fast there, cowboy," Eva said.

"I need a favor."

"Is that what you call it?" she chuckled.

I ignored her playfulness.

"I need a couple of your guys to go to my apartment."

"Wow, sounds kinky."

"Be serious, please. I just assaulted a cop and abandoned my apartment."

"Alright then," she said suddenly serious. "Why am I gonna have my guys stick their necks out? What's in it for me."

'That's more like it.' I thought as I stopped at a red light.

"There's some equipment in there that's quite valuable."

"And you want me to rescue it for you?"

"I want you to rescue the equipment yes, but you can keep it."

"What sort of equipment are we talking about, there cowboy?"

"A directional microphone, a high end surveillance camera, a laptop with listen and recording software, and a sniper rifle."

She whistled softly.

"Why are you trusting me with this equipment?"

"Because I have a feeling you know what to do with it."

"You're right there."

"And also I don't want it falling into the wrong hands."

"So you want to put your big gun in my hands?" she said slyly.

I swallowed hard.

"I don't want any kids getting a hold of that stuff, and believe me, I know if I'm not there the place will be robbed by tonight."

"And what am I exchanging for this mother load of equipment?"

"I need a safe place to gather my thoughts and decide on my next move."

"That's it?"

"I may need to use the place as a base of operations for a while."

"Define, 'a while'."

"I don't know at this point. It could be a week, a month, two months."

"I get it," she said and then was silent for a long moment. "I'm guessing you don't want it to be in my neighborhood."

"It doesn't matter what neighborhood it's in as long as I can hide my car and come and go as I please without being noticed."

"Hmm… Let me make a call and get right back to you."

"Ok."

I pulled away from the light as my stomach growled angrily.

"Yeah, I know," I said. "I was trying to get something."

As if an answer to my need a large yellow 'M' appeared in front of me.

"Bingo!" I said pulling into the drive thru and ordering a double burger meal.

I sat in the parking lot with my eyes peeled for cops and devoured my burger. I was just finishing the last gulp of soda when my phone rang.

"I have a place for you. Do you have GPS in your phone?" Eva said.

"Yes."

"Good. I'll text you the coordinates and the security code."

"Security code?"

"You know, to keep out unscrupulous people who may want to steal my things."

"That would never happen," I said sarcastically.

"It better not," she said then hung up.

I checked the text and entered the coordinates into my phone. The GPS led me out of town. It looked like I was heading towards the little town of Hayalet, when I took the last exit toward the airport. I followed the directions and turned onto Pitt road. I became concerned when the asphalt turned to gravel, but continued following directions. The road suddenly stopped at a battered old warehouse in the middle of nowhere. I got out and looked around. One of the outer markers for the airport runway was a stone's throw away.

I stepped up to the warehouse and found an old keypad beside the door covered by a rubber mat to keep it safe from the elements. I punched in the code and heard the lock click. I grabbed the knob and opened the door. The Inside looked bigger than the outside. I walked down the wall about twenty feet and found a pair of garage door openers hanging on a hook beside the garage door. I pressed the button and the door opened. I got in my car, drove it inside, and closed the door.

For the first time in a while, I felt safe.

My phone buzzed saying I got a text. It was from Eva.

'Once you get there you might want to consider turning off your GPS.'

'Good idea.' I thought.

I got out of the car and locked it out of habit. I decided to do a little exploring in my temporary home. There were six individual garages, each one of them locked. (I checked.) Beside the garages, was a car lift and racks of tools. Past the open car area was an indoor gun range with four stations and several lockers which I assumed held weapons. That area was cordoned off by reinforced concrete walls. Next was a recreation area, complete with pool table, ping pong table, and coin operated video games. Next to that was an exercise room complete with treadmills, weight machines, and stationary bikes. At this point the hallway took a right turn and led into the living room/dining room/kitchen open area. There was a massive TV on the wall that was almost as big as the wall itself. The dining room held a long rectangular table with ten chairs on each side plus one each at the head and foot.

The kitchen was a gourmet's delight. Everything you could possibly want was there. There was a walk-in cooler and freezer aside from the regular refrigerator which was stocked with food. Two ranges and ovens stood side by side along with a full table to work on.

I turned down the next hallway and came to the bedrooms. There were six in all, each nicely decorated completely in white, with a king-size bed, TV, closets, dressers, and its own full bathroom, but the master bedroom was above and beyond. It was completely done in red. The bed was shaped like a giant heart and there were mirrors on the ceiling. The bathroom was massive with a heart shaped tub for two. The whole thing reminded me of a honeymoon suite in Vegas.

I left that bedroom and chose one of the others for my own. I continued down the hallway and turned right again. This corridor had several doors that were all locked. The end of that hall led back out to the garage. I grabbed my go bag from the car and headed back to my bedroom. Once there I showered and changed into a robe I found in the closet. I went around to the kitchen and pulled out a steak and a beer. I took them back to my room, drank one and wore the other.

Before I drifted off to sleep I texted Eva, 'I'm home.'

'Don't get used to it,' she texted back. 'Remember it's only temporary.'

'Can't a guy dream?' I texted.

'You can dream about me,' she texted.

'I will.'

'Thanks for the toys by the way. Those will come in handy.'

'You're welcome. Now I'm gonna go to sleep and dream about this beautiful, mysterious woman I met yesterday.'

'Flattery, sir, will get you everywhere.'

She texted the wink emoji.

I smiled and closed my eyes.

***

I woke up in a strange room. I panicked for a moment before remembering where I was. I sat up so quickly the steak flew off my face and onto the floor. I quickly picked it up but it had left a red stain on the carpet.

'Great!' I thought. 'Guess I'll find out where the cleaning chemicals are today.'

I got up and changed from the borrowed robe into my clothes. I had a couple chores to do today. I found the cleaning supplies and returned to my room. I tried to clean the blood off the white carpet, but it still showed as pink. As a last resort I tried something I had heard once but never paid attention to. I went to the fridge and got a bottle of club soda. To my great surprise, it took care of the stain.

"I'll be damned," I said.

I took my go bag out with me to the kitchen as I made some breakfast. I sorted through my bag, pulling out my passports, my Beretta PX4 .40 caliber pistol, my Sig-Sauer .22 pistol with suppressor, two concealed throwing knives, and my cash. I counted it at $150,000. Then there were the other items. Two small cases that I had no need of opening right now. I knew what was in them and the situation wasn't that dire. I looked at the third small case, opened it and admired the ring inside. For a long time, I stared at the symbol on it. The gold shined in my eyes, pulling me into… I put it back in the case and closed it.

I steadied my breathing that was suddenly fast and shallow. I opened the case, grabbed the ring, and quickly stuffed it in my pocket without looking at it.

I put everything back in my bag except one of the knives and twenty thousand dollars. I kept my S&M

Shield 9mm in my conceal carry holster. I needed more ammo. That was one of my chores for the day.

After breakfast, I walked back down the stone road toward the airport. Two miles later I stepped into a dingy car lot that only had six cars out front.

"Good afternoon," a man said as he walked out of the office wearing a polyester suit and a greasy smile.

"How we doing today?" I said.

"Absolutely fabulous," he said. "What can I do to get you in one of these fine automobiles?"

I looked at his selection. Two Subarus, an old dodge pickup, a Saab, a Mustang, and a white cargo van.

"What's the story on this Mustang?" I said.

"That is one awesome driving machine," he said. "A true hot rod. This baby will plant you in your seat in a heartbeat."

I looked it over, finding lots of Bondo. When I tried to open the hood, he closed it right away.

"We don't need to see under there, this is an awesome car, let me start it for you."

He turned the key and the engine sputtered, finally roaring to life.

"There ya go, what'd I tell you?" he said over the sound of the engine misfiring.

"Yeah, it's something all right," I said. "How about this van?"

"It's just as solid as solid can be and a steal at only eighty-six hundred."

I checked around underneath, popped the hood, looked it all over without being interrupted once.

"I'll take it," I said. "I've got five thousand cash."

He licked his lips. "Did you say cash?"

"Yep."

I reached into my pocket and counted out five thousand dollars. He stared at it.

"I'm not sure I can go that low on this beauty," he said keeping his eyes on the money.

"I'll throw in an extra thousand if we do this with no paperwork."

He started drooling.

"You got yourself a deal."

I drove my new van to the local secondhand store 'Pop's plus'. It was a surplus store ran by a mean son of a bitch named Pop Rischer. Aside from Pop himself, the major identifying characteristic about the store was the front end of a World War 2 landing craft that was suspended over the entrance by some guide wires screwed into the face of the building.

Many of the people of Larsan believed it was going to collapse and kill someone someday. A majority of those people hoped that person would be Pop.

I filled my shopping cart with clothes, mostly t-shirts and jeans, with a suit thrown in for good measure. I walked up to the counter and emptied my cart.

Pop grunted at me before ringing up the clothes.

"Ammo," I said.

"What about it?"

"I need 4 boxes of .40 cal hollow points, 4 boxes of 9mm hollow points, and a 500 round box of .22's."

"Is that all?" he said sarcastically.

"No, as a matter of fact, I need 3 clips for a Beretta PX4 .40 cal, 3 clips for a Sig-Sauer mosquito, and 3 clips for a S&W Shield 9mm."

He glared at me then disappeared into the back room.

Ten minutes later he reappeared with all I had asked for. He rang up the items without making the mistake of asking if I needed anything else.

I paid him and walked out with 2 heavy bags of supplies.

As I pushed the door open, I nearly ran into Officer Morgan.

His face lit up when he saw me.

"Well, well, well, look who it is," he said pulling out his sidearm.

Twelve

I stood there, caught. My mind ran through a dozen escape scenarios, but none of them worked without someone getting hurt. He had the drop on me. My hands were both carrying heavy bags. There was no way for me to get to the concealed pistol in my waistband.

"I'm so happy to run into you, old buddy," he said grinning ear to ear. "I think you and I are gonna go around back and have a nice private chat."

I went with him to the side alley. No one bothered to follow or even look our way. They knew what was coming and didn't want any part of it.

"I think we got off on the wrong foot," I said putting down my bags. "Maybe I could make a generous donation to the policeman's ball."

He laughed. "Good one. I haven't heard that one in a while."

I slowly reached into my pocket and pulled out a wad of bills.

His eyes grew wide.

"Is there any way we can just forget we saw each other?"

He licked his lips and drooled at the wad of cash in my hand. He took the money and started counting it.

"So am I good to go?"

"Absolutely," he said.

I picked up my bags and started walking.

"You can go right into the back of my squad car," he said.

"But you took the money," I said.

He stuffed the bills in his pocket and said, "What money?"

I sighed.

"Well then you might as well have what's in this pocket," I said slowly reaching into my pocket and pulling out the ring. I slid it on my finger and showed it to him.

His look turned from triumph to disbelief to fear.

"No," he said. "You can't be."

I smiled as I showed him a secret hand signal and he grudgingly responded.

"So now am I free to go?"

"Yes," he said through gritted teeth.

I picked up my bags and started walking, then stopped and turned.

"One more thing," I said. "The money."

He opened his mouth like he was about to protest, then closed it, hung his head, pulled out the money, and gave it back to me.

"I was going to let you keep it if you let me go, but you pushed it too far."

"You're right, brother," he growled. "I pushed it too far, please forgive me."

"All is forgiven," I said putting my hand on his shoulder.

He flinched and I withdrew my hand.

"And do call off any search for me," I said.

"It will be done, brother."

"Thank you."

I walked away. As I turned the corner, I heard a long primal scream coming from the alley, followed by several gunshots that I hoped went into innocent garbage cans not innocent people. Passersby avoided looking down the alley and hurried past so as not to get involved. I got into my van and pulled away whistling a happy tune.

Today was a good day.

I grabbed some lunch and headed back towards the airport as it started to rain. As I turned off onto Pitt road, the engine sputtered. I milked it for all it was worth, but soon it died. Nothing I did could get it going again, so I gathered my bags and started walking. What started as a drizzle turned into a downpour. I held the lighter bag over my head in a vain attempt to keep dry as the water poured over me. One incredibly long mile later I walked up to the warehouse, input the code, and walked inside. I dropped my bags and stood there dripping. I took two steps toward my room and a dry robe, then froze. In an instant my gun was in my hand. Rain didn't concern me anymore. I was on full alert. There was a car parked beside mine.

I made my way through the building, eliminating one room after another. Finally, I came to the last unsearched room, mine. I turned the knob slowly and shoved the door in, jumping through and aiming my gun at the person on the bed.

Eva looked up at me.

"And here I thought I was the only one who was wet," she said.

I put the gun down and for the first time noticed what she was wearing, or maybe I should say what she wasn't wearing. She was dressed in a see thru teddy with a lace robe over it and she had high heels on. She was the most stunning woman I had ever seen. My jaw dropped.

She stretched, rose from the bed and walked over to me. She gave me a long deep kiss then said, "Why don't you go take a shower then come down to my room. I'm sure you know which one it is."

She sauntered out of the room as I caught my breath. I hurriedly showered, threw on a robe and headed for the red bedroom.

I knocked on the door.

"Really?" she said. "Yes, do come in."

I opened the door to a dimly lit room. The red had been augmented by the low lights. She laid on the bed on her side, one her breasts barely staying inside the teddy.

"Hello, stranger," she said. "Why don't you come over here and join me?"

I swallowed hard and stepped over to the bed, tripping on the rug and falling into bed. She laughed.

"I see you're falling for me now."

"I've been falling for you since we met."

She smiled and narrowed her eyes.

"So is this how you end up with all the women you're held hostage with?"

"Yep, every woman I've been held hostage with I've ended up right here."

She pulled me into a deep kiss.

"I'm glad."

I held her close kissing her neck and mouth. She grabbed my hand and pressed it against her breast. I obliged by squeezing and rubbing.

She rolled me over and mounted me.

"This is my rodeo and I'm in control," she said. "Cowboy."

"Yes ma'am," I said enjoying the view.

I'm very happy to say the rodeo lasted more than eight seconds, or even eight minutes. The fact is I have no idea how long it lasted, but it was amazing.

***

I woke an eternity later. Her eyes were already open and she was staring at me.

"That's not too creepy," I said.

"There's no reason it should be. Just because a strange woman you only met a few days ago is laying beside you naked, staring at you and running fingers through your chest hair. Why would that be creepy?"

I smiled and rolled toward her, wrapping my leg around hers.

"No reason at all," I said kissing her, which sent us into an overtime session of lovemaking.

When we were done, our naked bodies glistened with sweat. We laid beside each other, staring at ourselves in the mirrored ceiling.

"Wow!" I said.

"Wow is good," she said. "I wholeheartedly concur."

"I'm glad. I wanted to make sure you… " I blushed.

"Oh no, you don't have to worry. I definitely did. Time and again."

"Me too," I said.

"I do have one question though."

"It doesn't start with, 'Will you?' does it."

She laughed.

"Oh God no."

"Phew, that's good," I said not feeling the words.

"No, my question is who's Amelia?"

I froze.

"Who is who?" I said.

"Amelia."

My eyes widened in horror.

"Oh no, did I… ?"

"Yes, only once."

"I'm so, so, sorry."

"There's no need to be. It was so soft and sweet it was quite arousing."

"So, you're not mad?"

"Why would I be?"

"I don't know, because it's weird?"

"It's fine, I'm just curious."

I took a long, cleansing breath.

"Amelia is my wife."

"Your wife?" she said sitting up quickly and covering herself with the blanket.

"Was my wife," I said quickly. "She passed away giving birth to my daughter."

"The daughter you've been chasing?" she said.

"The same one."

"If it's not too personal, why did you think of your wife?"

I blushed.

"For a couple reasons," I said. "First is your eyes."

"My eyes?"

"Ever since the first time I saw your amazing eyes I've felt like I was looking into Amelia's."

She smiled.

"That's so sweet."

"The second reason is a little more embarrassing."

"Please tell me."

I sighed.

"You're the first woman I've... been with since her."

Her jaw fell.

"Are you serious?"

I nodded.

"How old is your daughter?"

"Twenty-three."

She stared at me for a long moment. Her eyes were in a turmoil, completely unreadable. I wasn't sure what she was going to do. And then she threw the blanket off and dove on top of me, pressing her body up against mine and kissing me even more passionately than before.

We were lost with each other. Nothing else existed except for us. We never heard the car pulling up to the building, the garage door opening and closing, the man and woman walking hand in hand, laughing and talking as they headed for the bedroom. All we heard was the door open.

"Eva?" Elliott said.

We both sat up and grabbed the blanket to cover ourselves.

"Hello, Elliott," she said.

"Elliott?" I said staring at his hand intertwined with Sharon's.

He immediately dropped her hand.

"Dad?" Sharon said. "I thought you were dead."

"Apparently you didn't do a good enough job of killing me," I said.

"What're you talking about?" she said.

"Don't try the innocent act, you never were very good at it," I sneered. "I know damn well you were injecting poison in my IV. I caught you at it."

"I don't know what you mean," she said looking away.

"Is this… ?" Eva said.

"Yes, this is my daughter that I've been trying to protect ever since she tried to kill me."

"Wait a minute," Sharon said. "You've been trying to protect me how?"

I didn't answer.

"By following you," Elliott said. "Taking out your dealers so you'd stop doing drugs."

"You're the reason no one will deal to me?" Sharon raged.

"You're welcome!" I screamed at Sharon. "And you," I said to Elliott. "How long have you been banging my daughter that's young enough to be your daughter.

He stood silent.

"Oh so you were complaining about her and how you wanted to get rid of her, all the time you two were playing hide the salami."

"You were complaining about me?" Sharon said to Elliott.

"As long as we're on the subject of banging," Elliott said glaring at Eva. "How long have you been at it?"

"Tonight was our first time, if you must know," Eva said. "I was rather hoping it wouldn't be our last."

She smiled at me and I smiled back.

"Oh, I'm gonna be sick," Sharon said.

"How charming," Eva said with a sarcastic grin.

"You're gonna be sick?" I said. "How about me? How about finding out the man I've known and trusted for years is secretly chasing after my daughter. How long has it been, Elliott? Were you scoping her out when she was in diapers, in middle school, did you wait as long as high school?"

Elliott stood silent.

"What about you?" Sharon said. "Keeping secrets like oh I don't know, how about, I'm alive."

"I pretended to be dead so you wouldn't make me that way," I said. "A fine payback for taking care of you all your life."

"So we're back on this? Your little prison of a life you enslaved me in?"

"You mean gave you everything you ever wanted?"

"Everything's my fault?"

"Yes, the drugs didn't do themselves," I said. "The money didn't steal itself. The poison didn't accidentally fall into my IV over and over. Yes, you, Sharon, are to blame. But you'll never admit that because that would mean taking responsibility, and we both know you'll never do that."

I was enraged. I was standing slowly coming toward her as I screamed. The blanket had fallen off, but I didn't care. In this moment, understanding just how much of a waste of skin my daughter had become, I had made my decision. There was no more protecting her. There was no innocence left to protect. I had wasted twenty-three years of my life on this creature that I no longer recognized as my daughter. I was coming to end her life.

Elliott pulled out his pistol and shot me in the head.

Thirteen

I floated for a while. Who knows how long. I was in blackness, drifting through bubbles of colors. Each one made a new pattern on me, like an easter egg being dipped into colors over and over again. The patterns swirled around me. I flew through space, dodging planets, racing comets, diving into black holes. Reality seemed to stretch out in front of me like a map showing the highlights of my life.

Images flashed through my head faster and faster.

My birth.

Walking for the first time.

Hitting my first home run in little league.

The first time I laid eyes on Amelia.

Our first kiss.

The awkward dates made so much easier by this wonderful woman.

The best day of my life when I walked Amelia down the aisle.

Sharon's birth combined with Amelia's death.

The blur that was single parenthood.

The pictures on the mantle crashing to the floor.

Sharon pulling the needle out of my IV.

The doctors calling my time of death.

The crosshairs on the forehead of the drug dealer.

My ridiculous disguise as I drove Sharon to the safe house.

Joe shaking me and telling me the police were on their way.

Meeting Eva.

The look on the crooked cop's face when I showed him the ring.

Making love to Eva.

Elliott shooting me in the head.

I woke with a start. I swore I could smell the gunpowder and feel the bullet enter my brain.

I opened my eyes and Elliott was standing over me.

I started screaming. "Help! Police! Murder!"

A nurse came running into the room.

"What's wrong?" she said.

"That man murdered me!" I yelled pointing my finger at Elliott.

She stared at me in shock.

"How could that be if you're alive?" she said.

"I'm telling you he shot me in the head!"

"But… " she said as I cringed away from Elliott as best I could in the hospital bed.

"I think he's confused," Elliott said. "I'll step out so you can explain things and maybe that'll calm him down."

Elliott left the room glancing over his shoulder.

"Keep him away from me!" I said.

"But he's been by your side most of the time you've been here," she said.

"Poisoning me like my daughter?" I said struggling to get up but not being able to.

"What are you talking about?"

"Don't play dumb," I said. "You're in with them, aren't you?"

"I'm not in with anyone but the hospital staff, sir. You need to calm down. This much exertion after being in your condition for so long isn't good for you."

"What condition? What the hell are you talking about?"

"You've been in a coma."

I stopped struggling.

"What do you mean a coma?"

"It started when you were rushed to the hospital with a heart issue and the ambulance got into an accident."

"But that didn't happen."

"Actually, it did."

"But I don't remember… "

"That's not uncommon in coma patients," she said. "Waking up can be a jarring experience."

"How long have I been… ?"

"Out? Months. They were able to fix your heart, but you were in a coma until just now."

"That can't be right," I said. "I remember having a heart attack, then the surgery. But then I was recovering and my daughter… "

"Your daughter what?"

I mumbled a response.

"I'm sorry, what?"

"She poisoned me."

"What? Sharon? That sweet thing? She brings us nurses coffee every day she visits. She's been by your side almost as much as Mr. Elliott."

"I'm sure she has."

"Why would she poison you anyway?"

"For my money."

"Do you have a lot of money."

"I will when I die."

"And you just assumed that your daughter tried to kill you to get your money?"

"Yes."

"I guarantee you that didn't happen."

"How can you be so sure?"

"Well first of all, you seem very much alive. And secondly you seem in relative good health. If she wanted to kill you the perfect time would've been when you were in a coma."

"But it seemed so real… "

"Did anything else happen in this dream of yours?"

"It wasn't a dream."

"Ok, tell me what happened."

"I found out Sharon was trying to kill me, so I asked Elliott to fake my death."

"You asked an insurance salesman to fake your death?" she said.

I tried to sit up but fell back to the bed.

"He's not an insurance salesman, that's his cover."

"So, he's what, a spy?"

"Something like that."

She rolled her eyes.

"Go on."

"After he faked my death I was able to recover and follow Sharon around."

"Let me guess, you're a spy too."

I looked around the empty room then curtly nodded.

"Ok," she said.

"I helped her get to a safe house after she killed one of her dealers."

"Dealers like cards?"

"Dealers like drugs."

"Sharon? No way."

"Anyway, I was helping her get to another safe house."

"What happened to the first one?"

"Elliott told me it wasn't safe."

"Right," she said sarcastically. "Because of bad guys."

She held up her fingers like a gun and pointed around the room.

"I got you covered," she said.

"It's not funny! It happened!"

"Ok," she said. "I'm sorry. Did anything else happen?"

"I kicked Sharon out of the car on the way to the safe house."

"Wait, why?"

"Because she tried to kill me again."

"Poison again?" she said with a grin.

"No, a gun this time."

"Ok, so your loving daughter tried to kill you twice, then what?"

"I went looking for her after I kicked her out."

"Second thoughts?"

"Something like that. But I got held hostage in a bad neighborhood, only to meet and fall in love with the most beautiful woman I've ever seen who happened to be the crime boss who grabbed me in disguise."

Her jaw fell open.

"Ok I've gotta go get some popcorn if you're gonna keep going. This is just too good."

"It's all the truth. It happened."

"I'm sure it feels like… "

"It wasn't a dream!" I yelled.

"Ok, I'm gonna go do my rounds and let you have some alone time."

She got up and left.

I knew they were working together, her and Elliott. The only thing I couldn't figure out was why.

I decided the smart thing to do was play along and wait for them to make a mistake.

There was a quiet tapping at my door. I looked up and saw Elliott peeking around the corner.

"Is it safe to come in?" he said hesitantly.

"Yeah," I said with a false grin. "The nurse defanged the wild bear."

"I'm glad," he said. "You had me worried there for a minute."

"Grab a seat and I'll regale you with all my memories that never happened before I go completely crazy."

"You're not crazy, buddy," he said. "Just confused. After being asleep for nearly three months, I'd be confused too."

He sat and I told him everything. All that had happened from the time I confronted Sharon to Elliott putting a bullet in my head.

"You look pretty healthy for someone who took a bullet to the noggin," he said.

"It's weird," I said rubbing a tender spot on my forehead. "It's like I can feel where it hit."

"That was from the ambulance crash," he said. "You've had that scar for a while. It's healed nicely compared to when you first got here."

"Was the driver ok?"

"The ambulance driver?"

"Yeah."

"He walked away with some bumps and bruises. The medic took a harder hit. She ended up with broken ribs and a concussion."

"Do you know their names?"

"It's been a while, I don't really remember, why?"

"I just thought maybe I'd send them a thank you/sympathy card for the whole ordeal just to save my old ass."

Elliott smiled.

"I'll find out for you when I go."

"Has Sharon been in to see me?"

"Only every day."

"But not inject anything in my IV tube," I chuckled showing I no longer believed what I believed now more than ever.

"No, she hasn't poisoned you," Elliott said. "And I don't think you should bring that up either. She's been very upset seeing you here every day. She was about to give up hope you'd ever recover."

'I'll bet she was'. I thought.

"I'm just so sorry to have caused her pain," I lied.

"Oh my God!" came an exclamation from the doorway as Sharon dropped the coffee she was carrying and put her hand to her mouth. "Is it true?"

She came over and hugged me so tightly I felt like my ribs would collapse.

"Ok, Sharon," Elliott said gently taking her arms. "Don't squeeze him to death because you're happy to see him alive."

Tears streamed down her face.

"I can't believe you're finally awake after all this time," she said.

"Here I am," I said.

"You won't believe the crazy dream your father had," Elliott said. "He dreamt he was a spy and I killed him."

"You?" Sharon said chuckling. "His best friend in the world who wouldn't hurt a fly?"

"Yeah," he said. "Can you imagine?"

"Not at all," she said. "That would be like watching a big teddy bear act like James Bond."

"Well, it's not too much of a stretch," I said. "I mean look at the size of this guy. I wouldn't want to meet him in a back alley."

Sharon laughed.

"Yeah, he might quote you actuarial tables to death."

I glared daggers at her. Elliott saw and tried to calm the rising storm.

"I don't know," Elliott said. "I guess I could be intimidating if I tried."

Sharon threw her arms around him and hugged him.

"Never," she said. "You'll always be a giant teddy bear to me as well as my godfather."

"Godfather?" I said.

"You remember," Elliott said. "When she was born you asked me to watch over her and be her godfather after Amelia… "

"Don't you say her name!" I said.

"Ok… " Elliott said. "I think maybe you need to rest a bit more. I feel like we've overwhelmed you enough for your first conversation in nearly three months."

"You ok, dad?" Sharon said taking my hand in hers.

I resisted the urge to pull away.

"I'm sorry," I said. "I think maybe Elliott is right. I'm just a little confused right now. Dreaming for months has me questioning reality."

"Just so you know, we always love you," she said leaning into Elliott.

"Absolutely, buddy," he said. "And don't worry, I'll find out those names for you."

"What names?" I said.

"The ambulance driver and the medic."

"Oh, right," I said. "Thanks."

Sharon leaned over and kissed me on the forehead.

"You just focus on getting better," she said. "And don't worry about anything. Elliott and I will take care of you."

I smiled and thought, 'That's exactly what I'm worried about.'

I held the smile until they left the room.

'Dammit!' I thought. 'What happened to the plan of going along? Way to raise suspicion by yelling at them.' I smacked myself in the forehead. It was more painful than I thought it would be. I felt along the crease of the scar where Elliott had shot me but he claimed it was from an ambulance accident. Had I really dreamed the whole thing?' Doubt crept into my mind.

'No! I know what happened. They're playing some game, I just don't know why. I have to do better at playing along and hiding my feelings.'

I eventually fell into a furtive sleep, unsure of my dreams.

I woke to a gentle knocking and saw Sharon peeking her head in the room.

"Is it safe to come in?" she said,

"Yeah," I sighed.

"Are you feeling any better?"

"A little," I said smiling. "I'm sorry for being a grump yesterday. I was just confused."

"You seemed like it."

"That dream seemed so real."

"Do you want to tell me about it?"

"Not right now," I said. "How are things going with you?"

"Well work is a little stressful at the moment."

"Flipping burgers is stressful?"

"Flipping burgers?" she said. "What are you talking about?"

"Your job."

"I work with you at the agency," she said. "Don't you remember?"

"The agency?" I said feeling panic rise in my throat.

"Yes, the insurance agency," she said. "Don't you remember you got me the job a few months ago?"

"Oh, yes, of course I remember."

"Translation, I don't remember but I'm too stubborn to admit it."

"Ok, you caught me. I don't remember you ever working at the agency."

"I started right before the accident."

I shook my head.

"Looks like I have a lot of remembering to do."

"Don't worry," she said holding my hand. "I'll help you."

I smiled. 'That's exactly what I'm worried about.' I thought.

Fourteen

Ted laid in bed eyes closed, snuggling with Alice. But he was far from asleep. Where had his serial killer disappeared to? Over the last month he had just vanished. Serial killers didn't just do that unless something happened. Maybe he'd run afoul of one of the drug dealers he was chasing. Maybe he'd been killed in a car wreck. It happened all the time. There were still murders every day. In a city of half a million people you couldn't go a day without a murder. But none of them fit the killer's profile. They didn't have that execution feel.

He'd tried getting the video footage from the grocery store on the night of the averted robbery, but the tape mysteriously went to static right before the incident and came back to normal after everything was over. He'd tried the outside camera to get a look at the guy's face and the same thing happened. He'd looked at every other camera around the neighborhood that might have seen something. None of them showed anything. And if there was a camera that looked like it would show something, it went to static right when he would've been able to see this guy.

Who was this guy, freakin Houdini? Was he an alien that interfered with cameras everywhere he went? Or was Joe covering his tracks? If so, why? What was Joe's connection to a serial killer? He seemed like a stand up guy. Someone who wanted to keep to himself and be left alone. Those usually aren't the kind of guys who will go out of their way like this to protect someone unless they have a close bond, like brothers. Was that it? Was Joe this guy's brother? It was time to find out.

Ted pulled his arm out from under his wife's head slowly. He slipped out from under the covers, picked up his clothes, making sure none of the metal doodads on his belt made noise, and snuck out of the room. The clock in his car read 11:37pm. He would have just enough time to get to the grocery store before Joe's shift ended. He parked in the same spot he'd used before where he could easily see the front as well as the back doors. This time he had the night vision binoculars with him. He scanned around the dark areas with them, trading pitch black for eerie green.

He scanned around the dumpster where he assumed Joe's friend had been the last time but there was no one there.

"Evening, Sheriff," Joe said in his ear causing Ted to jump. "Isn't it a little late to be hanging around in a dark parking lot?"

Ted took a measured breath to calm down before speaking.

"If you would just tell me who your buddy was, I wouldn't have to be here at all."

"What buddy is that?"

"You know exactly who. The guy who shot up your beer cooler and disappeared."

"Oh, that guy," Joe said. "I'd never seen him before that night."

"Just a good Samaritan passing through?"

"Apparently."

"Excuse me a second, by bullshit meter is going off."

Joe chuckled.

"What do you want me to say?"

"I want you to tell me who he is."

"I have no idea who he is."

"Ok, so you want me to arrest you on an obstruction charge?"

"And how would you make that stick?"

"Doesn't matter. I have reasonable suspicion."

"Despite the fact that I have cooperated with every other law enforcement agency?"

"Except this one."

"Why does this bother you so much?" Joe said. "Did this guy do something to you?"

"He broke the law."

"Yeah, and? People break the law every day."

"He's a serial killer."

Joe laughed.

"No, he really isn't."

"What about the trail of bodies he's left behind?"

"Whose bodies? Drug dealers? Killers? Anyone who will be missed?"

"That doesn't matter. He doesn't get to take the law into this own hands."

"You're right, Ted, no one should take the law into their own hands. How's your brother, Todd, by the way?"

Ted shoved on the door to open it and Joe shoved it right back closed.

"We're not gonna do that," he said. "I was just making a point. Everybody breaks the law."

Ted's face was red. He was fuming. His hand was on his sidearm and it was itching to serve this guy a lead salad.

"Ok, I can see we're done talking reasonable," Joe said. "I'll tell ya what. Since you've got such a hard on for this guy I'm sure you would've found him eventually. Here's his address. Go follow him around and you'll see he's just taking care of his own business."

Ted reached for the piece of paper and Joe pulled it away.

"Here's the kicker," Joe said. "You have to give him two weeks to show you he's a stand up guy. No arrest for two weeks. If after that you haven't seen him do anything illegal, you let him go. Let the whole thing drop and move on with your life. Deal?"

Ted eyed the paper.

"Deal."

Joe handed it to him.

"Have a nice night, Sheriff," Joe said walking away. "Give my regards to Alice."

Ted gritted his teeth and thought about arresting him anyway, but he was gone.

He looked at the piece of paper.

'Is it really that easy?' he thought.

He started the car then turned it off and went inside to get a gallon of milk. When he got home, he quietly snuck in the house to the kitchen. He didn't turn the lights on. He knew the house well enough he didn't want to risk waking Alice. On his way to the refrigerator he bumped into something. It was big and kept him from getting to the fridge.

The lights suddenly went on and it was Alice standing in front of the fridge.

"Jesus!" Ted said. "You scared the hell outta me."

She was standing with her arms folded in front of her chest. Never a good sign.

"Where were you?" She said.

"I wanted a snack but we were out of milk so I went for milk."

He held up the jug as if to show the evidence.

She eyed him suspiciously.

"That's all you went for is milk?"

"That's it."

"No stupid stakeouts?"

"No stakeouts," he lied.

"Ok, I'm going back to bed."

"I'm gonna get my snack."

She stopped halfway up the stairs.

"I've got something for you to snack on if you feel like it," she said then pulled off her robe and left it on the stairs.

Ted left the milk on the counter and ran up the stairs, picking up the robe as he went.

Fifteen

"I'll bet you're glad to be getting up out of that bed," the nurse said as she guided me on my daily walk.

"Actually, it's quite comfortable," I said. "I was considering another two-month nap."

"Seriously?" she said missing my sarcasm. "I don't think that would be very good for you."

I sighed and pretended to acquiesce. "Alright, I guess if you say so."

We made it to the end of the hall walking very slowly, then turned and walked back to the room. I had already been doing leg lifts, trunk twists, and arm stretches in my bed when no one was looking. I was just putting on the impression of still being frail and dependent on others.

"You're doing very well," the nurse said, trying not to be condescending but missing.

'I don't think she even recognizes it as condescension anymore,' I thought.

We feebled our way back to the room and I pretended to struggle getting into bed.

"At this rate you'll be home soon," she said.

"That'll be great," I said.

"And then your daughter can help take care of you."

I paused.

"Yes, that'll be awesome," I lied.

"You're not still worried about that silly dream, are you?" she said.

"No, of course not," I said, making a mental note to be extra careful around this nurse because she was quite perceptive.

She smiled and left as Sharon entered the room. 'Apparently I don't get a moments peace today.'

"Hi, sweetheart," I said plastering my best fake smile on my face.

"Hi, dad," she said kissing my forehead. "How are you feeling today?"

"Better. Making progress. I made it all the way to the end of the hall and back today."

"Super cool! You'll be ready to come home soon."

"Yep, looking forward to it," I lied. "So how was work?"

"Oh, you know, insurance," she said rolling her eyes.

"What, the fast-paced lifestyle of calling people and quoting numbers doesn't fit my thrill seeker daughter?"

"It pays the bills better than being a fast-food worker."

"Apparently it has its risks," I said. "What happened to your arm?"

She pulled her sleeve down over the scab on the inside of her elbow.

"Oh, nothing," she said. "I just slipped with a sharp knife the other day when I was making some supper."

"You might want to be careful," I said. "With a scar like that, people will think you're a druggie."

She laughed a little too loudly.

"That's ridiculous," she said. "I swear where do you come up with these things?"

"I'd like to think I brought my daughter up better than that."

"You did a great job of raising me, dad. I'd never even think about doing drugs."

"That's good because I'm still spry enough to kick your butt if you did," I said making a show of struggling to get out of bed, then falling back into it in apparent exhaustion.

"Yeah, you've got be shaking in my shoes," she said sarcastically.

"Watch the sass mouth, little girl," I said drawing my hand back to pretend to slap her face.

"You're funny," she said getting up.

"You're leaving already?"

"Sorry, I forgot I had some things to do," she said as she leaned over and kissed my forehead. "Love you."

"Love you too," I said as she walked out the door.

'Wow!' I thought. 'I need to mention drugs more often. Then I can have some peace and quiet.'

I leaned back in my bed and started doing leg lifts.

Two days later they released me into Sharon's custody and she drove me back to what used to be my house and now would be my prison.

She helped me in the door and I collapsed on the couch. I looked around and the place wasn't nearly as neatly kept as I had it. There were things out of place, a few soda cans on the coffee table, and the floor looked like it hadn't seen a vacuum in a while.

"I'm thinking this is gonna be my bed for a while, at least until I feel strong enough to handle stairs."

"How about some supper?" she said.

"What're we having?"

"I don't know. Let me check the pantry."

She disappeared but soon I heard muffled talking.

"Sharon?" I said.

No response.

I slowly rose and started toward the pantry. I listened at the door and heard more muffled talk. I ripped open the door and Sharon jumped.

"What's wrong?" I asked as she quickly put her phone in her pocket.

"Oh, it's nothing," she said grabbing a couple of cans off the shelves.

"I thought I heard someone talking."

"Talking? Oh right, Elliott called to see how things are going."

"That's funny, I didn't hear your phone ring."

"I've got it turned down so it won't disturb you."

"That's very considerate," I said. "So what are we having for supper. After months of hospital prepackaged food, I'm ready for a good home cooked meal."

"Oh, well we're having chicken noodle soup and tuna salad," she said holding up the cans.

"Sound good," I said not really meaning it.

We went back to the kitchen as she struggled to prepare the food. I don't know how she did it. You add water to the soup and heat it up. You add mayo to the tuna and serve it. Yet somehow she managed to make me miss hospital food.

I collapsed onto the couch wanting nothing more than to go to sleep, yet she insisted on watching a movie. She said she wanted us to have some father daughter bonding time together. I wanted no such thing, but I had to keep up the act. After yawning through the whole movie, she asked me if I was tired.

I swear these kids have no clue. She brought me my medicine that the hospital wanted me to take for a while after getting out. Finally, she went to bed and left me alone. I ran to the kitchen and spit out the meds I had cheeked. I grabbed a couple pieces of lunchmeat and ate them. Then I laid down and tried to get comfortable. The couch was lumpy and hard to sleep on. It was even worse than the hospital bed. I did my best to get a good night sleep, but it just wasn't happening. When she came out to the living room in the morning all bright eyed and bushy tailed I wanted to end the charade right then and tell her what I really thought of her before kicking her out. But I had a plan and needed to follow through if I wanted to find out what they were up to.

"I should stay home from work today so we can have some time together," Sharon said.

I inwardly cringed.

"Why would you do that when we can hang out together all evening," I said.

"But we could do things together we haven't done in years, like take a walk in the park."

"Honestly, I think I'll be sleeping most of the day. I didn't get much sleep last night."

"Oh, why not?"

"Just getting used to being home I think."

"Ok, if you really want me to, I'll go to work."

"How about a rain check when I'm feeling a little better?"

"Deal," she said. "Are you sure you'll be alright alone?"

"I'll be fine, thanks. I'll probably have a bowl of cereal later."

"Ok," she said kissing me on the forehead. "Love you, you get lots of rest. Maybe we can play board games tonight."

"That'd be great," I said showing my best fake smile.

She grabbed her purse and car keys and headed for the door.

"Drive safe," I said.

As soon as the door closed my fake smile disappeared. I waited for 30 seconds before I went to the window and saw her pull out of the driveway, talking on her phone. I sprinted for her room and checked for her stash. I reached up to her hiding place in her closet, but there was nothing there. No box, no needle, no lighter, nothing.

'She must've moved it,' I thought.

Next, I went to the secret compartment upstairs in my bedroom floor that had my backup go bag in it. But there was a problem. There was no secret compartment. I tried over and over to open it, but it just wasn't there. There was no impression in the boards that I always used to press on to make the latch appear. The boards were totally smooth, like they had always been that way.

'That can't be,' I thought. 'I know this is where it was.'

In desperation, I went to the basement where my main stash of weapons and money lay under an inch of concrete. I found the small sledgehammer and moved the table and chair to the side to uncover the place I had buried the chest. I grabbed the sledge, raised it over my head and...

"What are you doing?" Elliott's voice boomed.

I nearly dropped the hammer.

"Are you trying to give me a literal heart attack?" I said grabbing my chest.

"Sorry, buddy, didn't mean to scare you, but heaving a sledge over your head like that I thought you were gonna hurt yourself. What were you doing anyways?"

I thought as quickly as I could.

"There was a spider."

"And you chased it into the basement with a sledgehammer?"

"It was a big spider," I said not having any other excuse pop into my head.

"How about we put the hammer down and go back upstairs and I'll make you a cup of coffee?"

"Ok," I said dropping the hammer and going back into my feeble act.

I stumbled up the stairs. Elliott caught me and helped me the rest of the way up to the kitchen.

"Here, you have a seat and I'll make the coffee," he said guiding me to a kitchen chair.

"Thanks," I said, dropping into the chair.

He went to the exact place where the coffee was, pulled out the coffee maker and started brewing a pot. When it was done, he brought me over a cup as well. It already had milk swirling around in it.

I smiled. "You remember how I take my coffee."

"Yep, milk and sugar," he said.

"And you're straight black with one of the pink sweeteners."

"You got it," he said.

"Then why do I have these other things mixed up?"

"You were in a coma for a long time," he said. "It's hard to tell what kind of effect that can have on your mind."

As if on cue my world started spinning.

"Whoa," I said grabbing the table. "What did you put in that coffee?"

"Milk and sugar, just like I said, why?"

"I'm feeling dizzy."

"That's not good. Do you need to lay down?"

"Maybe I should," I said starting to get up then falling back into the chair.

"Hold on. Let me help."

He came around the table and practically carried me to the couch. I was reminded just how large and strong this man was. I started thinking of ways to disable him when the time came I had to fight him.

He gently laid me on the couch and covered me with a blanket.

"Thanks," I said still feeling the room tilting.

"Maybe I'll sit here for a while and make sure you're ok."

"Don't you have to work?"

"You know our job. I can make some calls this afternoon and catch up."

The chair groaned under his weight as he settled into it.

"How about some TV?" he said picking up the remote.

He turned it on and immediately I recognized the movie Goldeneye. James Bond was talking to the man he thought was his friend all along.

James told Alec he trusted him and Alec told him trust was a quaint idea.

"Maybe we could watch something else," I said.

He flipped from channel to channel. Every scene seemed to be about a close friend betraying another.

"Maybe you could turn it off and I'll just get some sleep," I said.

"That's fine," he said turning the TV off. "I'll catch up on my schedule for this afternoon."

'And I'll lay here and worry about the person who betrayed me murdering me in my sleep,' I thought.

Sixteen

I woke up alive and somewhat surprised to be so. I was alone but it was still light outside. I looked at the clock and it read 3:10. Sharon would be getting home in a little over an hour. I still felt a little dizzy. Did Elliott really put something in my drink or was I having aftereffects of being in a coma? It seemed like my belief in the treachery of my friend and daughter was taking a beating by harsh reality. The drugs I couldn't find in her room, the hidden compartment that had disappeared, both of them treating me like a sick child rather than a mortal enemy. A pattern was starting to emerge with only two plausible conclusions. Either they were telling the truth and I dreamed the whole thing, or they were putting on one helluva show covering it up.

Three days ago I would've bet the farm, the town, and the whole county on the latter. But lately my resolve had been chipped away. Now I was riding the fence. My stubbornness could only hold out for so long against overwhelming facts.

What happened to the jaded agent of the agency that would do anything without hesitation to complete the mission? Was any of that true either? How much of my life was a self-imposed lie? Was I really an agent of the company trained to kill without hesitation? Or was I just an ordinary everyday insurance agent who had a vivid dream and latched onto that reality because it was infinitely more interesting than the forced boredom of a career selling insurance?

It seemed so real though. If only I had some shred of proof. But every bit of evidence I searched for seemed to turn to dust before my eyes. I pulled out my phone and looked for Eva's number. It wasn't there. Yet another nail in the coffin of my denial. I heard the car pull in and got an idea.

"Hey, dad, I'm home," Sharon called.

"Dad?" she said when she didn't see me. She crept into the kitchen slowly, looking carefully all around.

"I'm here," I said jumping out from behind the fridge.

"Oh, Jesus," she said clutching her chest. "You scared the crap out of me."

"I'm sorry," I lied. "I'm just feeling a bit more spry this afternoon. In fact why don't we go for a drive and pick up some supper?"

"That sounds nice, but I just got home and was planning on some couch time."

I gave her the pouty face look.

"Please?" I said.

"Oh ok," she said.

"Great, I'll drive," I said grabbing the keys.

"What? No. You just got out of the hospital. I'll drive."

"Fine," I said holding up the keys for her to take.

We got in the car and buckled.

"Where would you like to go?" she said with weary eyes.

"How about we go downtown?"

"Downtown? For what?"

"Just to look around," I said. "I haven't seen the old neighborhood in years."

"You're the boss," she said starting the car.

"And don't you forget it, young lady," I said with a smile.

She sighed and turned left onto the highway headed into Larsan. After a few miles she saw the first signs for Larsan exits.

"Why don't we go see the stadium, dad?"

"What for? A bunch of overpaid babies getting millions to play a kid's game? Pass."

"Wow. Don't mince words, tell me what you really think."

"That was the G-rated version of how I feel about professional sports."

"Ok, switching topics," she said as we passed the sign that said, 'Next exit, home of the Larsan Lancers.' "I don't ever remember living in downtown Larsan."

"It was before you were born."

"You've never even mentioned it."

"There's lots of things I've done that I've never told you."

"Oh really?" she said with a sideways look. "Such as…?"

"Such as if they were any of your business, I would've told you already now keep your eyes on the road, or you'll miss our exit."

She straightened in her seat. I knew that had rattled her, but she didn't mention it.

"So which exit is ours?"

"Zahn Avenue."

"Zahn Avenue? What's down there?"

"I don't know. Let's go see."

She opened her mouth, I assume to protest, but then shut it again as she turned onto the ramp leading to Zahn Avenue. Traffic was bumper to bumper, which I knew she hated. It wouldn't take long before she would give up on the charade and turn back.

We ran with the traffic for blocks. Sometimes we got going pretty good, and other times we slowed to a crawl. With each traffic light I could feel her tension growing. The skyscrapers flanking us on both sides made the road ahead look like a giant metal canyon and we were trying to flow with the river of humanity at the bottom of it.

As we drove further south the buildings grew shorter and dingier. The gleaming metal was replaced by brick, then concrete, and finally wood. When we passed 51st street, there were only tenement buildings.

"Have we gone far enough?" she said with an edge in her voice.

"Just a bit farther," I said not telling her our real destination. I wanted to see her reaction.

She passed 60th street and got dead quiet. It seemed like her hands were glued to the wheel and her knuckles were white.

"Can we please go home?" she said quietly as if the people on the street might somehow hear her, become offended, then transform into a mob of zombies and attack the car.

Come to think of it there were a few people walking the sidewalks that could already qualify as zombies. The guy in five layers of ragged coats pushing an old shopping cart, the lady talking to the empty leash as she dragged it along behind her, the man holding a sign that announced the end was near, but it looked like both him and his sign had been the victim of graffiti.

But the one thing I didn't see was the people leaning against the streetposts. Eva's people who I had nodded to the day she let me go. We passed 63rd street and I saw it coming up.

"Stop!" I said.

She slammed on the brakes and looked around for what had made me yell. As soon as she did, I jumped out of the car.

"Dad!" she yelled. "Dad! What are you doing?"

I crossed the street, dodging drivers that were blowing their horns and offering very colorful interpretations of my family tree with special attention to my parentage. I ran towards Eva's apartment, sprinted up the stairs, and knocked on the door.

It flung open and there stood the big guy who had kept Eva captive in the basement.

I smiled. "I need to talk to Eva."

He wasn't smiling in the least. His huge body filled the entire doorway.

"Who's Eva?" he said.

"You know… Eva, your boss."

"I don't know what you're talkin' about, but ain't no Eva here."

He stepped inside and swung the door to close it as I jumped in the doorframe and blocked it open.

"Please, I need to talk to her," I said.

He pushed me out through the door effortlessly.

"There ain't no Eva here," he said. "Now get your skinny old ass off my doorstep or Mr. Glock and I are gonna have a discussion with you."

He pulled out a Glock and showed me the barrel.

My arm was yanked down the stairs.

"I'm so sorry, sir," Sharon said as she pulled me toward the street. "My father hasn't been feeling well. We didn't mean to disturb you."

He watched for a few seconds as she dragged me to the car and shoved me inside, then he stepped back in the apartment and slammed the door.

The chorus of horns continued as we pulled away, turning left on 64th street, then left again on Harrison Street. She drove in silence as we reversed our descent into darkness. It wasn't until we passed 43rd street that she said anything.

"So that's what this was all about?" she said. "You're still trying to prove that your dream was real. That Elliott and I are trying to kill you?"

I looked over and tears were streaming down her cheeks.

"You really believe it don't you?" she said. "That the two people closest to you want you dead."

I didn't say anything.

"Right now, I can't say I don't," she said. "In fact, maybe I should just pull out my gun and take care of you right now."

She reached under the seat. I froze. Time slowed down as I ran through possibilities. Jumping out of a car going 45 wasn't a healthy option. But then lead poisoning wasn't really high up on the survival list either. She pulled her hand out from under the seat and I grabbed her arm hoping to keep it pointed away from me until I could disarm her.

Her hand was empty.

I looked over and her other hand was on the wheel.

"I don't have a damn gun in my car because I'm not trying to kill you!" she screamed at me.

She pulled over, jumped out of the car, and started power walking. I jumped out and had to run to catch up with her.

"Sharon," I said but she ignored me and kept on walking.

"Where are you going?" I said.

"I don't care, as long as I'm not near you!"

"What do you want me to say?"

"Nothing. You've said it all by risking our lives to prove your point."

"I'm sorry, ok?"

She kept walking.

"I said I'm sorry!"

"I heard you the first time. I wonder if you meant it either time or if you said it a hundred more times would you mean it?"

"What do you want from me?"

She stopped so quickly I nearly ran into her. She grabbed my coat and pushed me against a wall.

"I want my father back!" she screamed. "I want the man who loved me and took care of me my entire life. The man who was always there to pick me up when I was low. I want him back. But you know what, you're right. I think he died in that hospital bed. I don't know who woke up that day but it wasn't my dad."

She looked into my eyes, streaks of makeup ran down her face from crying, but her look was as hard as steel.

"Tell me you're not that person," she said. "Tell me you're my father who loves me and not this paranoid maniac who came home with me."

"I… I'm sorry," I said bowing my head. "I'm sorry for putting you through this. I'm sorry for suspecting you. I'm sorry I've taken all your love and sympathy and flushed them down the toilet of suspicion. I'm sorry you didn't have a mother to love you. I'm sorry you had to put up with my pathetic attempts at being a single parent."

Tears broke from my eyes and rolled down my hot cheeks. I was carried away by a pent up sea of emotion. I slid down the wall to the ground. She hugged me and rocked me as I sobbed like a baby.

Seventeen

For days Ted sat in his car across the street from the address he'd been given. Two weeks. That's what Joe had said. Watch him for two weeks and if he doesn't do anything suspicious leave him be. Ted grudgingly had accepted the conditions and was prepared to honor them no matter how much he felt it was wrong. Ted's gut told him this was the guy. This was the serial killer he'd been looking for.

Unfortunately, it seemed like Joe would get his way. It had only been three days he watched as the guy sat on his couch and watched TV. His daughter would go to work and come home, and they would sit around the house. Ted was considering nominating him for world's most boring human.

It was day four and nothing had happened. Ted sighed in frustration.

"Son of a bitch," he said starting his car and putting it in gear.

Just then the man and his daughter came out of the house and got in the car. He looked like a dog who had been told they were going for a ride. He bounded to the car, got in and fastened his seat belt. Ted considered driving away, but decided to follow along.

"Where the hell you going?" Ted said as they turned onto Zahn avenue and headed south.

Ted became more uneasy the farther they went into the wrong part of Larsan. He had kept a three-car distance between them and was trying to remain inconspicuous, but in traffic this heavy there was no need. He followed them into the darkest part of the city. The buildings had deteriorated into a morass of broken homes that he imagined held broken people.

He was starting to worry when suddenly they came to a screeching halt. He jumped out of the car and Ted had to slam on his brakes to not run him over.

Ted slid into the nearest parking space he could find as other drivers went around him, screaming all kinds of colorful names at the lunatic who had run across the road.

Ted watched as he ran up to one of the apartments and knocked on the door. Ted pulled out his cell phone and snapped a picture. After a brief encounter with a mountain of a man, his daughter pulled him away and back to the car. He surprisingly walked away unharmed but visibly dejected. Ted made a note of the address to look into later. He also watched as the daughter read him the riot act while they turned around and headed back out of town.

Ted followed simply because he was headed back out of town too. When they pulled over north of 45th street, he pulled over and watched out of curiosity. He felt like a voyeur watching father and daughter have a bonding moment as someone stole their car.

He considered calling it in but how would he explain how he happened to be watching as it happened. Instead, he went to the station and checked in for the first time this week.

He went to his office and tossed his notepad on the desk. Papers and cases had piled up in his absence. He sighed and was about to dig into his neglected duties when he noticed the address he'd jotted down on the pad.

He looked it up in his computer and found it was the address of a suspected drug dealer.

Click

That's what it sounded like in Ted's head.

'Serial killer who kills only drug dealers knocking on the door of a suspected drug dealer.'

Ted smiled.

"Gotcha."

He headed to the grocery store where Joe worked. He couldn't help but notice how close it was to the drug dealer's neighborhood.

"Whatcha know, Joe?" Ted said walking in the door.

Joe glared at him.

"What are you doing back here?" he said. "I told you everything."

"I don't think so. How about we start again? Who's Eva?"

"Who?"

"Sorry, the dumb routine isn't playing anymore."

"Look, I told you where the guy lived, what else do you want?"

"Everything. I followed him downtown today to a suspected drug dealer's house."

Ted pulled out his cell phone and showed Joe the picture he'd taken earlier.

"Yeah, and?"

"Ok look, you tell me the whole story or I'll run you in on an obstruction charge," Ted said pulling out his cuffs for emphasis.

The three people in line behind Ted watched with a growing interest as though a soap opera was unfolding in front of them.

"That'll never stick," Joe said.

"I'm sure it won't but I can still hold you until you get a lawyer and get out on bail, probably five thousand or so. Can you afford that as a store clerk?"

Joe's face was stone but his knuckles were white as he clenched his fists.

"Just tell him what he wants to know," one of the waiting customers said.

He looked back at the line that had grown to six people, all waiting impatiently to purchase their items, but also paying close attention to the conversation between him and Ted.

"Fine," Joe said. "I'll take my break in ten minutes and tell you what you need to know."

Ted stepped out of line and waited beside the counter making Joe angry.

After ten minutes another clerk relived Joe and he walked outside with Ted.

He pulled out a cigarette and offered Ted one.

"You're a persistent son of a bitch," Joe said.

"That's what my wife tells me."

As Ted reached for the cigarette, Joe swung a massive roundhouse punch that connected with Ted's temple. Ted crumpled to the ground. He sat there dazed for a moment trying to shake away the stars.

He recovered and slowly got up looking around for his assailant but Joe was gone. He hobbled around to the front of the building still trying to get his bearings, but no Joe. He went back inside but he wasn't there either. Joe had disappeared.

Eighteen

Sharon and I held each other for who knows how long, rocking back and forth, both of us crying. People walked past by the hundreds without even noticing us. An eternity later I pulled away, looked in her red puffy eyes and kissed her forehead.

She smiled, then laughed.

"Maybe we should go home," Sharon said standing to her feet.

She reached down and offered me a hand.

"What, don't you think your old man is as spry as he used to be?" I said feigning insult.

"You kept up with me pretty good for a man who was in a coma last week," she said pulling me to my feet.

"I may or may not have been in somewhat better shape than I let on."

"Really? I never would guessed," she said her words dripping with sarcasm.

We started walking back to the car much slower this time.

"I was thinking," she said after a few minutes. "Maybe since you're so good at acting now we could get you involved in an all seniors play at a local nursing home."

"Wow!" I said. "That was below the belt."

She chuckled.

"You deserved it."

"Yeah, I did. Maybe I could go to Hollywood and get a part on a daytime soap opera?"

"You probably could with acting chops like that."

She hugged me and we laughed.

"There's my dad," she said.

I stopped.

"What's wrong?" she said.

"Were's the car?"

She turned and followed my stare. Sure enough, there was an empty space where she had pulled the car over.

"Do you remember locking it?" she asked.

"I don't remember if you even closed the door."

We looked up and down the street, but the constant flow of people and cars made it impossible to pinpoint anything especially our car.

"You've gotta be kidding me," I said looking at her.

She looked back at me, and we both started laughing.

"That's our lives to a 'T' at the moment," she said.

I glanced across the road and saw a sign that said, 'Dan's Diner'.

"Come on, I'll buy you some lunch," I said pointing out the sign.

"With our luck I hope we don't end up with food poisoning," she said.

I chuckled but not wholeheartedly.

"Relax, that was a joke," she said.

I smiled all the way to my eyes to let her know I was ok.

We crossed the road, which was an adventure in itself, and made it into the crowded diner. It was on the waning side of lunch rush but in the city that still means standing room only. It took fifteen minutes for us to get a table. We sat and looked over the menus when an attractive middle-aged waitress came over.

"How we doing today?" she said.

"Well, we just had our car stolen," Sharon said.

"Oh dear. Did you call the police?"

"Not yet, we wanted to get some lunch first."

"Ok, I guess priorities."

"Your name sounds familiar," I said looking at her name badge that said, 'Ellyn'. "Are you famous or something?"

"No, not me, if I were would I be working here?"

"Good point," I said. "Just out of curiosity, what's your last name?"

She stiffened.

"It's Watkins," she said. "Would you excuse me, I have another table that needs my attention."

She hurried off but not to a table. She went towards the back where it looked like the bathrooms were.

"I've got it," Sharon said.

"Got what?"

"Ellyn Watkins, she's Billy Watkins mom."

"Who's Billy Watkins?"

"You remember a year or so ago when that kid took on the Pro Football Association?"

"Oh yeah," I said brightening at putting the memory together.

"You remember what happened?"

"Oh yeah," I said darkening at the bad memory.

"It's no wonder she took off. She didn't want to be reminded. I bet people do that to her all the time without even thinking about it."

"Should I go apologize?"

"No, I think maybe we should just go I'm not really hungry anyways."

"Alright, I'll call the police if you hail us a cab."

Forty minutes later we pulled into our driveway, much worse for wear. Between running, crying, and screaming, we looked like we had gone fifteen rounds in the ring, not to mention the cab ride from hell which is another story altogether.

We walked up to the door, unlocked it, wondering if we hadn't been robbed while we were gone. I walked inside and there stood Elliott with his arms crossed in front of his chest tapping his foot.

"And where have you two been?" he said looking very intimidating.

"We went for a drive," I said. "Chill out, 'dad'."

"Where's the car?"

Sharon and I looked at each other.

"It's a long story," she said. "I'm too tired to tell it right now."

She plopped on the couch and pulled her shoes off with her feet.

"What about you?" he said.

"I'm with her," I said plopping on the couch and trying the same thing with my shoes but failing and having to pull them off with my hands.

"So what happened today?" he said.

"Captain stubborn here decided he wanted to take a road trip," she said. "Let's just say it didn't end up the way he thought it would. Which was a good thing. We got some things figured out."

She smiled and took my hand.

"We sure did."

"So all's well that ends well, I guess. Even if it ended with the car getting stolen," Elliott said. "And did you think to call your insurance agent about that?"

I whipped out my phone and dialed a number. Immediately Elliott's phone rang. He answered.

"Hello?" he said.

"Hey, Elliott, the strangest thing just happened," I said. "You're not gonna believe it."

He hung up.

"Smartass," he said with a smile.

"So since we don't have a car," Sharon said. "What are we gonna do this evening?"

"I say we order a pizza and watch a movie."

"What are you, fourteen?" Elliott said. "Besides, I'd rather play videogames."

We all started laughing. It was the best I felt in a long time. It's strange how the way you think about things can bring you down. I was probably headed for a second heart attack with the stress I was putting myself under by sneaking around pretending to be some secret agent and trying to find out what my daughter and best friend were up to when they weren't up to anything except taking care of me.

We laughed and carried on as we played video games, drank beer, and ate pizza. It was the happiest time I'd had in forever. It carried over into the next day and the day after that. I started getting up early and taking a morning jog with Sharon. It was invigorating and cleared my head. We had chats as we went and found we had a lot more in common than either of us thought.

I went back to work and found fulfilment sitting at a generic desk, crunching numbers. The insurance even came through and got us money for a new car. I almost hate to say the words for fear of jinxing it, but it seemed like the happy ending of my story was achieved.

We settled on a used Ford Fiesta until we could find a better second car.

Now if only I could find Sharon a man I could trust with my little girl, my life would be complete.

***

I sat at my desk staring at my computer when my cell phone rang.

"Hello?" I said.

"Are you available?" a raspy voice said.

"Available for what?"

"I got a deadbeat that I need cleared out. Can you and your guys get here this afternoon?"

"What guys? I'm sorry but who is this? How did you get this number?"

"This is Robbie, the super from over on 60th street. You gave it to me, remember, you and your crew came a few months ago and cleaned out that girl's apartment?"

"What was the girl's name?"

"What was it? Let me think for a minute," he said. "Oh yeah, it was Sharon, Sharon Bishop."

My veins turned to ice. I looked across the room at my daughter sitting at her desk talking on the phone.

"You remember me being there and emptying the apartment?" I said slowly.

"Oh yeah, you and your guys did it up real quick. I got another deadbeat that needs to be vacated in a hurry. I remember you guys did such a good job I wanted to see what your rates were."

I stared at the phone. The mountain of lies my daughter and best friend had told me for months came crashing down in my mind and all that was left was a massive smoking crater that was the truth. They had tried to kill me. It was all true.

"Hello?" Robbie said bringing me back to reality.

"I'm sorry... Robbie was it? I'm all booked up at the moment. Maybe if you give me your number I can get back to you in a few days."

"Alright, sounds good."

He gave me the number as my mind was a thousand miles away.

"I'll get back to you ASAP," I said. "And Robbie..."

"Yeah?"

"Thank you. I really mean that."

"Umm... you're welcome?"

Nineteen

I stared at the demon I had spawned sitting there on the phone trying to pretend she was selling insurance. My mind spun like a helicopter blade. Part of me wanted to pretend I didn't know the truth. I wanted to see how long she could keep up this charade. I mean if she's pretending to be clean she's gotta be clean, right? I think that would be the worst torture for her. To know that she can't do drugs or it'll blow her cover.

And what about Elliott? The man who's been a spy for as long as he's been my friend. Which of course begs the question was he ever my friend or was I just a means to an end? I could play it cool and let them slip up. But that didn't work out so well the last time. No, I needed to dig deep into myself and put on a mask that not even I would recognize as deceit.

I needed to also be vigilant. I needed to be ready. And I needed help.

A plan started coming together, but it would require subtlety, precision, and patience. I took a walk during my lunch break. Next to the food court in the building was a stand that sold prepaid phones. I bought one and dialed a number I would never forget.

"Yes?" Eva said on the second ring.

"There's a word I haven't heard you moan in a while," I said.

"Who is this?"

"I think you know."

"The only thing I know is I'm about to hang up."

"When was the last time you rode a cowboy?"

The line went silent.

"I know, Eva," I said. "I know everything. They tried to convince me it was a dream but I found out the truth."

"I have no idea who you are or what you're talking about, goodbye."

"Wait, please don't hang up yet," I said. "There's one more thing I can say that might convince you."

"I'm listening."

"Amelia," I said quietly.

I heard a quick intake of breath.

"Sorry," she said. "I can't help you."

"I understand."

The line stayed open for a few seconds. I thought I heard her start to say something but then she hung up. I looked at the phone and smiled. It was more than I hoped for. She had told me all I needed to know and I had an opening.

It was Tuesday. On Wednesdays I followed up on leads. Which included calling and/or visiting prospective clients. Sharon knew this and drove to work alone the next day. I called an Uber and rode to a perspective client's house. After I was done I took an Uber to the edge of town. I had them drop me off out by the airport where Pitt road began. I walked down the gravel road for a mile before I came across an abandoned van on the side of the road.

I smiled as I remembered the day it left me sitting here. Just one more confirmation of the truth. As I continued toward the warehouse I wondered how much trouble and expense Elliott and Sharon must've gone to. Reboarding the floor in the house must've been expensive. I smiled at the amount of money they'd wasted. Then I thought again. It was probably my retirement and insurance money they had used. That turned my good mood sour.

I kept on toward my destination, seeing the top of the warehouse. I made sure no one else was around before I approached the keypad and tried the code she had given me. I wasn't surprised when it didn't work. I pulled out my phone and texted Eva.

'I'm at the place we were together last. I need the new code to get inside.'

'You can't be there,' she texted right back.

'Why? I need my things and my car.'

'I don't know if someone's there or not.'

'No, he does office hours on Wednesday.'

There was a long pause.

'4,7,3,9' came the answer.

I typed in the code and the door opened. I stepped inside and was struck by empty space.

'Where's my car?' I texted.

'In the second garage. The code is 6969.'

'Nice. Any chance of you and I doing that anytime soon?'

There was a very long pause as I opened the garage and found my car. I got the hide a key and opened it up. I popped the trunk and found the secret compartment with a go bag in it. A quick search found a berretta and a stash of cash around 50g.

'I don't think that would be a good idea,' she finally texted back.

'Just curious,' I texted. 'Where's my stuff?'

'In the back seat of your car.'

I looked and sure enough there was my second go bag along with a pile of nicely folded clothes.

'Thank you,' I texted.

'You need to get out of there.'

I did exactly as she said, driving my car out, closing up and wiping down everything I had touched like I was never there. I drove quickly down the gravel road and parked behind the used car lot where the salesman sold me a lemon of a van. I took up a stakeout position and watched the road.

'Are you still there?' Eva texted.

'No.'

'Okay, please don't go back there again.'

'The only reason I would go back is for you.'

Long silence.

'You should lose this number.'

'Thank you for helping me.'

'You're welcome… Cowboy.'

I smiled from ear to ear as I started my car and drove to town. I rented a storage unit on the other side of town from the house. I parked the car inside and left my go bags there. I had checked and everything was still there, including my ring and the two small boxes, along with close to two hundred thousand dollars. I left it all in the car including the guns, clothes, and ammo. Now wasn't the time. I needed to plan and get things together before I executed anything… or anyone.

I took an Uber home and got there just before Sharon. I put on my 'happy, oblivious, daddy' face and smiled as she walked in the door.

"How was the daily grind today?" I said.

"Not bad," she said. "I can't wait for the time when I get to spend a day out galivanting around the countryside like you."

"Oh you'll get there. You need to build up your client list first."

"Got any extra clients you wanna get rid of?"

"I could think of a couple," I said looking at her. "But then you wouldn't learn your lesson."

"What?"

"I mean you wouldn't learn how to get your own clients."

"If I even stay in insurance. I've been thinking about something more exciting."

"Like what?"

"Nursing."

"Really?"

"Just think of it. All those people I could help."

'All those drugs you could steal... ' I thought.

"That sounds like a great idea," I said.

"You really think I should?"

"Absolutely, I think it's what you were meant to do."

"Wow. I thought you'd be disappointed that I'm not following in your footsteps."

I hugged her.

"You've shown me exactly how much I've misjudged you and how much I can trust you."

She squeezed me.

"Thanks, dad. I so glad you're back to your old self."

I smiled the biggest smile I could fake.

"Me too."

Twenty

Ted slammed his car door shut.

"Dammit!" he said starting it up and heading back to the office.

He had visited the store again looking for Joe and found out he had quit.

"Back to square one," he said.

He drove north watching, hoping for any excuse to arrest someone. He left the neighborhood frustrated.

"What the hell?" he said. "Are all the drug dealers and muggers taking the day off?"

He continued up Zahn avenue when he passed the spot where the father and daughter had stopped and had their love-in the other day. He shook his head in frustration thinking how many dead ends he had run up against in this investigation.

"Am I fooling myself?" he said. "Is this really worth all the time and effort, not to mention the stress on my marriage. All for what? To catch some guy who's killing drug dealers?"

He came to the crossroads. Turning left would take him back to the office, turning right would go towards his quarry's house. He stopped at the intersection. He looked left then looked right. The car behind him honked his horn. Ted glared in his mirror at the impatient driver. He considered arresting the guy, but instead turned right and hit the gas. His tires squealed and he started to slide sideways. He eased off the gas and regained control. As he started toward the outskirts of town his eyes narrowed and his resolve hardened.

He pulled into a very familiar driveway that he had watched for days. He took a deep breath, got out of the car, and walked up to the door. Three knocks later, the door opened.

"Can I help you?" the man said.

"Mr. Bishop?" Ted said.

"Yes?" he said.

"I'm sheriff Secrest, may I come in?"

"Umm… sure," he said opening the door. "Is there anything wrong?"

"I'm following up on your stolen vehicle report," Ted said stepping inside and looking around.

"That was fast," he said closing the door.

"I happened to be in the area."

"Can I get you anything?"

"No, I'm good."

"Ok."

"Wait," Ted said. "On second thought, could I bother you for a glass of water?"

"Sure thing."

He pulled a glass out of the cupboard, filled it with water from the sink and handed it to Ted.

"So, what can I do for you, sheriff?"

Ted took a long drink then sat at the kitchen table and pulled out his notebook.

"You reported that your car had been stolen?"

"Yes."

"Where was it when it was stolen?"

"Across the street from Dan's diner."

"Down on 43rd in Larsan?"

"Yes."

"Was the car locked?"

"Umm... no."

Ted scribbled in his notebook.

"Were the keys in it?"

"Yes, they were."

Ted looked over at Mr. Bishop then scribbled some more.

"Don't you think it would've been a good idea to take your keys with you and lock your car?"

"We were having a moment."

"We?"

"My daughter was in the car with me."

"Oh, who was driving?"

"She was."

"What kind of a moment were you having?"

"A personal one."

Ted scribbled.

"So, your daughter and you are driving down the road in the middle of Larsan traffic. She decides to pull over so you two can have a moment and doesn't lock the car or take the keys?"

"It was a very emotional moment."

"Does it have anything to do with where you had stopped earlier?"

"And just where had we stopped earlier?"

"Don't you remember?"

Ted scribbled.

"What exactly am I supposed to remember?"

"Why don't you tell me? What were you doing in town anyway?"

"Going for a drive. Is that illegal?"

"That all depends on what you do before, after, or during the drive."

"Would you mind clarifying for me exactly what you're implying?"

"Well, if you're say for example, going to kill someone, then the drive would be highly illegal."

"Kill someone? Like who?"

"It's a dangerous place you were driving around in. A lot of drug dealers have gotten themselves killed down there recently."

"Are you implying I'm a drug dealer?"

"No, I'm not," Ted said leveling his gaze at Bishop.

"What are you saying then?"

Bishop narrowed his eyes at Ted.

"Hello?" Sharon called as she walked in the front door.

"In here, sweetheart," Bishop called.

"Why is there a car in the… " Sharon said walking into the dining room and seeing Ted. "Oh, we have a guest."

"Sheriff Secrest, ma'am," Ted said standing.

"Hello, sheriff, what brings you by?" she said.

"The sheriff was following up on our stolen car report," Bishop answered quickly.

"Oh, I didn't know there would be an investigation," she said. "I thought the insurance company would take care of it."

"That's not my only reason for stopping by, ma'am," Ted said. "I'm also looking into a recent string of murders."

"Murders?" she said taking an involuntary step toward the door. "What would we know about any murders?"

"I don't know, ma'am, I was hoping you could tell me," Ted said flipping a few pages in his notebook. "Didn't you used to have an apartment in Larsan?"

Her eyes shot to her father, then Ted, then the floor.

"Umm… I don't recall."

"You don't recall living at 1301 60th street?"

"It's possible, why?"

"There was a murder committed in that apartment."

"I don't know anything about any murder," she said looking at the floor. "Who was the victim?"

"We don't know."

"Then how do you know there was a murder?"

"There was a report of a domestic disturbance. A woman that matched your description and a man. He pulled her into a building and a short time later she emerged alone, got in to an uber, and drove away. The man was never seen again."

"How do you know it was a murder then?" Bishop said. "Maybe the man was just sleeping something off."

"Because he never emerged," Ted said. "When the scene was investigated, they found nothing."

"I'm confused," Bishop said. "You say there was a murder, then you say there was no evidence of a murder."

"I believe the evidence was cleaned by a professional."

"Who would do something like that?" Bishop said.

Ted's eyes bored into Bishop's. "I wonder," he said.

"Excuse me," Sharon said, "I have to go to the bathroom."

She quickly went back the hall, leaving Ted staring at her father.

"I heard you recently had a couple hospital stays," Ted said.

"Where did you hear that?"

"Where do you think I heard it from?" he said eyes intently focused on Bishop.

"I don't know. That kind of information isn't common knowledge."

"Maybe from the admissions desk," he said. "Or maybe from your friend, Joe."

Bishop's breath hitched.

"Joe?" I said. "I don't know anyone named Joe."

"Really?" Ted said. "Because I know around a dozen Joes. But this one happens to work down at the grocery store on the corner of 60th and Stone. You remember, the one you where you shot the beer cooler?"

Bishop mustered every ounce of fortitude not to react.

"What else did my alleged friend have to say?"

"Quite a bit," Ted said as he reached down to his belt and pulled off a set of handcuffs. He set them on the table and playfully spun them. "We had quite a long conversation about you."

Bishop tensed thinking about the gun in his waistband and how much trouble it would be to clean up the mess. Mostly he thought about his plan and how Sharon and Elliott had finally bought his not remembering act. To do anything rash would destroy months of work.

"You caught me, sheriff," Bishop said holding out his wrists. "I admit I shot that cooler trying to save Joe and his store from a couple of thugs. I admit to fleeing the scene. Take me in. Isn't that you wanted?"

Ted eyed Bishop's wrists.

"Who said I was here after you?" he said his eyes drifting to the hallway where Sharon had disappeared.

"What's she done?" Bishop said.

"I'm sure you know," Ted said turning his eyes back to his wrists.

"I'm sure I don't," he said. "If my daughter was a murderer, I'd like to think I'd know."

"Would you?" he said twirling the cuffs once more. "What were you in the hospital for the last time?"

"I was in a coma and don't remember a lot of that visit."

"A coma caused by what?"

"It varies depending on who you talk to."

"Really?" Ted said raising an eyebrow. "The doctors didn't tell you why you were there?"

"If they did, I don't remember. It was a confusing time."

"I'm sure," he said. "Did your daughter visit you in the hospital?"

"Yes, she was there every day."

"But you're not confused about that?"

Bishop sipped his drink.

"Did anyone else visit you in the hospital?"

Bishop looked Ted dead in the eye and lied.

"No one."

Ted smiled, stood up, and grabbed his cuffs off the table. Bishop held his breath as he waited for Ted to order him to stand. Instead, he finished his drink then snapped the cuffs back on his belt. Bishop stared at the cuffs dangling from the belt as he started for the door.

He tipped his hat as he stepped out, then paused.

"Be seeing you," he said.

Bishop watched, stunned as he walked down the driveway, got into his car and left.

***

Ted smiled as he drove down the street heading towards the station. He carefully took the glass out of his pocket and pulled open the evidence bag that was laying on the passenger seat. He placed the glass inside. In his minds eye, he could already see the fingerprints he would use to run a nationwide search on Mr. Bishop.

He was looking forward to the results.

Twenty-One

"What am I supposed to do?" Sharon said into the phone as she paced in the bathroom.

"What exactly is he accusing you of?" Elliott said on the other end of the call.

"He mentioned about the man I killed in my apartment," she said as she turned on the sink for cover noise.

"Did he say he was charging you?"

"No."

"Did he say he was going to question you?"

"No."

"Well, what did he say?" Elliott said, trying to contain his impatience.

"He said they had a report of a domestic disturbance with a man and a woman matching my description. He said that people saw us go inside but only me come out."

"Did he say they had the body?"

"No, he said there was no body."

"Then how could they accuse anyone of murder?"

"That's what dad said."

"Did he seem surprised by the sheriff's questions?"

"I'm not sure," Sharon said. "I was in full panic mode at that point."

"It's important," Elliott said tersely. "Think, did your father seem like any of this was a shock to him?"

"I think so, why is that so important?"

"Because if he wasn't surprised that means he knew about it and he didn't believe our story about the coma."

"That would be bad."

"It would also mean that he's been playing us," Elliott said.

There was a knock at the door and Sharon jumped. She lost her grip on the phone and it fell onto the rim of the toilet. She dove for it, but instead of catching it, she knocked it into the bowl.

"Shit!" she said as she stared at the cell phone sinking to the bottom of the toilet.

"Honey, are you ok?" he father said from the other side of the door.

"I'm fine, thanks," she lied.

"Ok, well I'll be here when you come out."

"Is the sheriff gone?" she said.

"Yes, he left a few minutes ago."

She opened the door a crack.

"Is he going to arrest me?"

"He didn't say he was," her father said. "Is there any reason he should?"

"Of course not," she said trying to sound nonchalant.

"That's good," he said. "What was all that stuff he was talking about?"

"I have no idea," she lied. "But he was starting to sound like he was looking for someone to take the blame for it."

"I understand how that could make you upset," he said. "It's awful when someone tries to set you up for something you haven't done."

She gazed into his eyes looking for any indication of what he was thinking.

"Well, I didn't want to disturb you," he said. "Just wanted to make sure you were ok."

"I'm fine," she said smiling. "I'll be down soon."

He pulled the door closed and she collapsed against it.

'He knows,' she thought.

She stood and went over to the toilet, then sighed and stared at the phone with revulsion. She was tempted to just flush it, but she knew what Elliott would say. 'We can't have any evidence laying around.' She grimaced at the thought of sullying herself for something as stupid as this. The longer she glared at the phone the more she knew there was no choice. She reached her hand into the water and pulled it out. She tried to dry it off but knew there was no saving it. She left it sitting on the sink counter, glaring at it as though it was to blame for all her troubles.

Sharon came back down to the smell of tomato sauce. Her father was making spaghetti for supper.

"You need any help?" she said.

"You can set the table if you want."

A few minutes later there was a knock at the door. Sharon froze, not sure if it was the sheriff coming back or not. She slowly walked up and opened the door. Elliott stood there. Sharon grabbed him in a massive hug.

"Not now," Elliott hissed pulling her arms off him as her father came to the door.

"Who was at the... oh, hey Elliott. How's it going?"

Elliott plastered a fake smile on his face.

"Great, how are you doing?"

"I'm fine. I'm making supper you want to stick around and eat with us?"

"What're you having?"

"Spaghetti," he said.

"That's my favorite," Elliott said. "I think I might stay, if you have enough."

"I'm sure we'll manage. It's almost ready, come on in."

Bishop walked back into the kitchen while Elliott and Sharon did a comical dance of her trying to hold him and him trying to push her away.

They went to the table and Elliott sat down. Sharon immediately sat beside him and pulled her chair as close as possible. Elliott grimaced and pushed her chair away with his foot. She gave him a wounded look and he mouthed the words, 'Not now!'

Bishop came in carrying a steaming pot of spaghetti and set it down in the middle of the table.

"I forgot to get you a place setting," he said and disappeared back into the kitchen.

"Later I promise," Elliott leaned over and whispered in her ear. "But not here with your father watching. We don't know if he knows or not."

Elliott sat up just before Bishop came back in the room.

"Here we go," he said setting a plate, fork, and glass in front of Elliott. He also brought out garlic bread and set it beside the spaghetti.

Bishop sat down, folded his hands, and closed his eyes.

"Dear Lord, thank you for this day. Thank you for the many opportunities we've had to help others and thank you for your forgiveness. For we know that on our own we can never forgive anyone, but only through you can we truly forgive those who have done terrible things to us."

Elliott opened one eye and shot a look at Sharon. Her face seemed unperturbed by her father's prayer. Elliott sighed inwardly and closed his eye.

"Thank you for this food," Bishop continued. "And thank you for the company of those I wish to keep closest to me. Amen."

Elliott shot a sideways glance at Bishop.

"I didn't know we were getting a sermon with supper," he said taking a big helping of spaghetti.

"I guess I'm just in a thankful mood," Bishop said, filling his plate. "After our close call this afternoon."

"What close call?" Elliott said.

"The sheriff showed up and was making all kinds of crazy accusations. I'm surprised Sharon didn't tell you."

"Why would she tell me?" Elliott said, feigning ignorance.

"Oh, I just assumed she was on the phone with you earlier."

"No," Elliott said at the same time Sharon said, "Yes."

Bishop looked between them.

"Should I leave you two alone to figure it out?"

"Yes," Sharon said at the same time Elliott said, "No."

"O… K… " Bishop said with a forkful of spaghetti paused halfway to his mouth. "You know what, I think I'm gonna go take a walk to stretch my legs and work up an appetite."

He looked over at Sharon who had a desperate look in her eyes.

"Or maybe I'll go for a drive," Bishop said. "A long drive."

He got up from the table, grabbed the car keys and walked out the front door.

The door had barely shut until Sharon was all over Elliott. Her hands were everywhere. She ripped off his suit coat and had his shirt halfway unbuttoned before he grabbed her hands and held them.

"Slow down," he said. "We need to talk about your father."

"What about him?" she said, struggling to get loose from his strong hands.

"Does he know what's really going on? Does he know we lied to him about the coma?"

"Who cares?" she said. "I want you right now. We can talk about him later."

"He could come back at any minute."

"What about the words 'long drive' didn't you understand?"

She yanked free from his grip, stood and took off her clothes.

"If you like what you see I'll be in my bedroom waiting."

With that she strutted away.

Elliott enjoyed watching her bare behind wiggle. He sighed heavily knowing why she was acting like this. The more nervous she was the hornier she was. It's why so many drug dealers gave her slack. They knew all they had to do was make her nervous and they were in for a helluva time. The night Bishop dropped her off at the safe house she was naked 30 seconds after he let her in.

Elliott stood, left his jacket on the chair and started up the stairs.

Twenty-Two

"You've gotta be kidding me!" Ted said to the computer.

The computer didn't answer back. It just continued showing the same information, 'Classified'. Ted ran the prints through every agency he knew, they all came back the same, 'Classified'. None of them came back 'Unknown' just 'Classified'. Which meant they all knew who this guy was, but no one would tell him. He was seriously considering committing computericide when the call came in. There was a house fire. Ted heard this same call hundreds of times during his career, but what made him pay attention to this one was the address. He had just left there.

He grabbed his hat and broke every speed record getting back to Bishop's house. When he got there, he found Sharon standing outside near and ambulance covered in a blanket with her arm around a behemoth of a man.

He walked up to her.

"Are you alright?" Ted said.

"What do you care?" she snapped.

He turned to the man and extended his hand.

"I'm sorry, we haven't met, I'm Ted Secrest."

"Elliott," the man said squeezing his hand.

Ted fought to keep the pain off his face until Elliott released him.

"What happened?" Ted asked Sharon.

"We were having a barbeque and things got out of hand," she said.

"Really?" Ted said.

"No!" she said. "I was being sarcastic."

"Where's your father?" Ted said.

"I have no idea," Sharon said. "I thought maybe you had arrested him."

"The last time I saw him was when I left here."

"We don't know where he is," Elliott said.

"Have the firemen been in the house looking for him?"

"Yes, repeatedly," Elliott said. "They have yet to find anything."

"If you'll excuse me, I'm going to go wait in the car," Sharon said glaring daggers at Ted.

Ted and Elliott watched her storm off.

"Was it something I said?" Ted said.

"She's naturally upset with losing her house and her father in the same night," Elliott said.

"Naturally."

"Plus, I think you might have upset her earlier."

"Why would she be upset if she didn't do anything?" Ted said, turning to Elliott.

He shrugged. "You know how some people get upset when they even see a cop. Their imagination runs wild. They think of every little thing they've ever done and wonder if it's coming back to haunt them."

"What about you?" Ted said.

"Me? I'm clean as a baby's behind."

"I meant what do you think happened here and was it connected to my visit earlier?"

Elliott looked down at his shirt.

"That's funny," he said. "I don't have a badge on my shirt."

"Alright wise guy," Ted said. "No reason I can't ask a few questions."

"Ok, I have no idea what happened here. I have no idea where Bishop is, and I have no idea why you're harassing Sharon. Good enough?"

"Sounds suspiciously like, 'no comment'," Ted sighed. "But yeah, that'll do."

"Do you have any more questions for her or me?"

Ted thought for a moment.

"None that I can think of right now."

"Then why don't you do your job, sheriff? Go find my friend."

Elliott lumbered to his car and drove away with Sharon in the passenger seat.

Ted stood and stared at the glowing embers that were the house he'd questioned Bishop in just hours earlier. He stared with an intensity that seemed like the fire would give him the answers he wanted. Unfortunately, they didn't. After a few minutes of fruitless staring, Ted found the fire marshal and asked him to forward a report on the cause of the fire. Then Ted drove home frustrated and needing some answers. Instead, he got the usual questions from his wife. 'Where were you? Why are you so late? Did something happen?'

This neediness was really starting to grate on him. He knew about the traumas in her past but why were they suddenly surfacing and with such vigor?

When they laid down in bed for the night, she latched onto him like a lovesick octopus. She didn't want to do anything though, just hold him.

Ted sighed heavily and turned out the light. It wasn't fifteen minutes until the phone rang. He reached for it but she pulled him back.

"Please just let it ring," she begged.

He gently pulled her loose and answered the phone. The fire marshal gave him the news he suspected. It appeared that the fire had been set deliberately. He narrowed his eyes, thanked the marshal, then hung up the phone and rolled back into bed. Alice had rolled to the other side. She didn't try to hold him, just pretended to be asleep.

Ted rolled away from her and fell asleep. He never saw the tears streaming from her eyes. Hours later she finally fell asleep.

Twenty-Three

I lied to Sharon and Elliott. I got in the car and drove away all right. But I never had any intention of going for a drive, at least not right away. One block away from home, I pulled over near a grove of trees and parked the car where it wouldn't be seen. I snuck back to the house knowing what I would find.

As I approached, I saw the lights go out in Sharon's bedroom. I tried to keep the image of Elliott and my daughter out of my mind. I thought for a moment. This could be my chance. I snuck into the house, ignoring the sounds coming from upstairs, and grabbed some cleaning supplies from under the sink. I snuck into the basement and searched for my tools. I got an old desk lamp that was sitting on my workbench and clipped just enough of the shielding off the wire to make it spark. Then I set up the rest of my firebomb.

I made it look like the lamp had fallen to the floor on top of some old rags that had paint thinner on them. Once I got the fire going, I quickly left, knowing I'd be back. I stared at the middle of the floor. The smooth concrete covered my real objective.

I continued out of the house, stopping to look back once I had made it to the tree line. The smoke was starting to pour out of the basement windows. I wondered if I should've paid Sharon and Elliott a visit while they were otherwise occupied and knocked them out, leaving them for the fire to devour.

No, I still wanted answers. As dangerous as they were, I wanted to know why the deception started. I snuck away to my car and drove off. It was time for that long drive. I made sure I stopped for food I didn't want and gas I didn't need to make sure I had witnesses and an alibi.

***

I returned the next day under cover of night. I knew Elliott and Sharon would be wearing masks of concern, but I needed to get something before I let them know I was still around. I parked in the same grove of trees and snuck up to what was left of the house. I ducked under the police tape and approached the pile of rubble that used to be my house. I cleared away the detritus as quietly as possible, working my way down to the basement.

I found the spot, covered it with a heavy blanket and began pounding with my sledgehammer. It wasn't as quiet as I wanted but at least not as loud as naked steel on bare concrete. Fifteen minutes later I had worked up a sweat. I dug away the chunks of concrete while checking my surroundings to be sure no one had heard me. Once cleared, I opened my trunk to reveal the treasure within.

I was greeted by some old friends. Two pistols, plus one with a silencer, an automatic rifle, an Uzi, and plenty of clips for each. I loaded them into my duffle bag then pulled the section of the trunk out to get into the bottom. There was a lot of cash, and a small metal box. I stared at the box for a long time, knowing what was inside but not wanting to open it here. I placed it carefully in the duffle bag, along with the money, tucked the silenced pistol in my waistband then heaved the bag over my shoulder, and started the climb out.

I was greeted by the neighbor's dog. A chocolate lab who was doing all she could to help me by licking my face. A flashlight assaulted my eyes as the dog's owner came over to see what his dog had dug up.

"Who's there?" the neighbor said.

"Just me," I said thinking about using the pistol in my waistband.

"Oh, hey, what're you doing here?"

"Well, it did used to be my house, so… "

"Yeah, I understand, digging out precious mementos?"

"Something like that," I said hefting the bag and hoping the barrel of the rifle wasn't sticking out.

"Too bad about the house," he said.

"Yeah, it's been home for a long time," I said feeling a tug of remorse.

"Any idea what caused the fire?"

"Nothing I can think of," I lied.

"Do you think you'll rebuild?"

"Not sure," I said truthfully. "I may take the chance to travel. I might even retire."

"Wow! Anyplace you're thinking of going?"

"Back," I said with a far-off look.

"O… K… ," my neighbor said. "Well, I'm gonna get going, you have a nice evening."

"You too," I said coming out of my trance.

I took my supplies and hefted them back to the car. Once inside I locked the doors and counted the cash. It came to $500,000. I put it back in the bag and pulled out the small box. I looked at it with a mixture of anticipation and fear.

I put it aside for the moment. I needed to get myself together before Elliott and Sharon started searching for me in earnest. I drove to my storage unit and loaded my stash in my Charger, then headed to town to find a place that was suitable.

Twenty-Four

The plane was losing altitude fast. The pilot struggled with the non-responsive controls. He had called air traffic control, but they didn't answer. The electronics had been knocked out by the lightning strike. He wrenched the wheel with every ounce of strength he had but it wasn't enough to keep the plane level.

The unconscious copilot was no help. With the electronics out, he couldn't announce on the intercom for the passengers to fasten their seat belts or get into crash positions.

The altimeter was spinning like a fan, but the numbers were going in a bad direction. If they were going up the ride would be exhilarating, but since they were going the other way they were merely counting down to the deaths of all 157 people on board.

He would've liked to have his life flash before his eyes instead of the flashing of lights and numbers on bunch of useless instruments that were all telling him the same thing. 'You're about to die'.

The lights of the city were clear and becoming clearer by the second. Helplesness overwhelmed him as he continued his futile fight to regain control of the plane that was heading toward destruction. He stared out in terror, trying to decide which and how many buildings were about to be victims of the giant tube of death that was hurtling toward them.

The first building clipped the left wing just beyond the engine. The impact ripped the section of wing off, causing the plane to list to the right and start into a flat spin.

It collided with building after building, each tearing away a part while sacrificing its own pieces of glass, steel, and brick. It all combined for a rain of death on the streets below. People looked up for an instant then ran for cover once the horror that descended on them sunk in. Even though it was bleeding airspeed the plane still had enough momentum to keep aloft. But the fight with gravity was almost lost. It flew a mere hundred feet off the ground now and the collisions with the buildings had taken its toll. It was heading for the ground fast, right in the middle of the busiest street in Larsan.

It hit the ground with massive force, throwing cars and streetlights hundreds of feet in the air. It dug a deep trench in the asphalt causing sparks to shower the ground. Unfortunately, the fuel tanks had already been damaged and were throwing jet fuel in every direction. Physics doesn't take a day off. It doesn't take a timeout. The sparks did what they are meant to do. They set fire to any flammable object they touched. It was only a matter of time until the first one landed in a pool of jet fuel. The reaction was immediate and devastating. The fire caught up with the plane and engulfed it. The outer parts of the wings had been shorn off, leaving only the engines. The fuselage had somehow remained intact, which in the end was a bad thing.

The plane had finally lost its inertia. However, it was now engulfed in flame, trapping the passengers in a giant metal oven. Interviews with witnesses later said that they could hear the screams coming from inside as the passengers were roasted alive. Some bold soul managed to open the escape door, but the fire was too great. Instead of giving them the hope for life, it doomed them to death. The oxygen masks still dangling from the ceiling had made the interior an oxygen rich environment. The flames were drawn to it like a magnet.

Within seconds the interior was engulfed with fire made ravenous by the oxygen. It tore through like a rushing wind. No one was safe. As people on the street recovered and tried to help, the fire reached the fuel tanks. The explosion was beyond devastating.

It took fire trucks an hour to get within range to control the blaze. Neighboring buildings had caught fire and burned down as they helplessly watched. The death toll was in the hundreds, approaching thousands, and growing by the hour. It would be weeks until all the bodies were unearthed from not only the plane, but the cars in the street that were destroyed on impact or burned. And then there were the helpless souls in the buildings just going about their daily business, not knowing it would be their last day alive.

In the midst of all of the carnage, no one paid any attention to a burned up Ford Fiesta that laid in the rubble of the plane's path of destruction, belonging to Martin Bishop.

Twenty-Five

"No," Sharon said, shaking her head. "It can't be true."

"I'm sorry, ma'am," the officer said. "We found the car in the wreckage of the crash. We took DNA samples of the body inside and they matched with your father."

"You're wrong," she said. "It's a trick. He's done this before."

"I'm sorry, maybe I misunderstood you," the officer said shaking his head. "You're saying he somehow faked being run over and burned up by a plane?"

"I wouldn't put it past him."

The officer looked to Elliott for help.

"Unfortunately, it's true," he said. "Her father wasn't well. He liked to play some sadistic games."

"Umm… ok, well this isn't a game. He's gone. I'm very sorry."

The officer turned and walked away shaking his head.

Sharon buried her face in Elliott's chest and he took her inside. Once the door was closed she looked up at him. Tears streamed down her face.

"I can't believe it," she said.

"Me neither," Elliott said. "I thought you hated your father."

She pushed away from him.

"Of course, I hated him," she said. "But that doesn't mean I didn't love him."

"That makes no sense."

She turned away and crossed her arms in front of her chest.

"I wouldn't expect you to understand," she said.

"Understand what?" he said. "That the one thing we've wanted all along has finally happened and you're acting like it's the end of the world."

"Maybe it is."

His mouth fell open.

"I need some Tylenol," he said rubbing his temples as he went to the kitchen.

"What do we do now," she said, following him to the kitchen.

"What do you mean, what do we do now?" he said, opening the bottle of pain relivers and dumping two into his massive hand. "We put on some black dress clothes, wear hang dog expressions at the funeral, then collect the life insurance money."

"You really think he's dead?"

He washed down the pills with a swallow of water, then slowly set the glass on the counter.

"I honestly don't know. If they say they found his DNA in the wreckage… "

"Could he have faked it?"

"Of course he could've, but how could he fake getting hit by a plane?"

"You worked with him all those years; you tell me."

"I mean, it's possible, but so many people were killed that day. If he was caught in traffic when it crashed, there would've been no place for him to go. Two whole city blocks turned into an inferno. He'd have nowhere to hide."

"So, this is actually it?" she said. "No more looking over our shoulders to see if he's coming after us?"

"Seems like it."

She turned and walked away.

He let her go, putting the bottle of pills back in the cabinet. He walked into the living room of his apartment and saw the curtains flowing in the breeze. He walked over and found her out on the balcony, leaning on the rail and looking over the spectacular view of Larsan city.

He stood beside her silently, enjoying the warm mid-September breeze as he scanned the horizon. They were only a block over from where the plane had exploded, and they could see some of the wreckage.

"I just can't believe it," she said, staring at the remnants of the wreckage and the cleanup crew doing their monumental task.

She leaned her head onto his massive shoulder.

'At least now he'll never know my secret,' Elliott thought.

The End

(For now)

Bonus chapter, sneak peek at Ties (Book 2)

One

The machines beeping were starting to wear on my nerves. They were incessant. Even over the cacophony of movement and orders being given and received, there was that incessant beeping.

A constant reminder of the seriousness of the situation.

My hand hurt, but that was all. It was because my wife had been squeezing it off and on for the last few hours as she lay in the hospital bed in labor.

We were both so happy and proud months ago when the doctor announced that she was pregnant. I could never imagine being any happier with my wife or my life until that moment.

I looked down at her lying in the bed, her brow wet with perspiration that had run down and soaked into her gown. She was exhausted, but still radiant.

My happiness began to fade as the general mood of the room turned more urgent. Medical terms started drifting around that raised my concern.

'Breech birth.'

'Emergency procedure.'

'Survival rate.'

I retained the words and filtered them for my wife when she became concerned.

"What's happening?" she said, barely able to speak above a whisper from exhaustion.

"They're doing all they can, sweetheart," I said, squeezing her hand for encouragement. "Everything's going to be fine."

She smiled weakly.

"I can't wait to get our baby home," she said. "Promise me you'll always take care of her."

"Of course, I will," I said. "We both will."

She opened her mouth as if to say something, then closed it again.

"I love you," she said, then closed her eyes.

The incessant beep turned to one long tone.

"Babe?" I said, trying to rouse her.

She didn't move.

"Get a crash cart in here!" a doctor yelled.

"What about the baby?" a nurse said.

"We've got to get her out."

"Sir, I need you to step outside, please."

"Why?" I said, as the orderly ushered me out of the room. "What's wrong?"

"We need the space to work if we're going to save your daughter."

"But what about my wife?"

"We're doing everything we can," he said as a cart was wheeled past me and into the room.

I tried to follow it inside but the orderly pushed me back out.

"Sir, wait here."

I reluctantly watched as they surrounded my wife working fervently. I was disturbed by the amount of blood I saw on the gloves and gowns of everyone in the room. Had it been that much before and I just hadn't noticed?

For what seemed like eternity, they worked until I heard the wail of a baby.

My heart soared hearing my child alive and well, until I saw they weren't working on my wife anymore. The machine still blared out its monotone beep. I couldn't take it, and pushed through the door.

"What about my wife?" I yelled. "Why aren't you trying to save her?"

"Sir, we're doing what we can," one of the orderlies said.

"No, you're not, no one's even looking at her. You saved the baby, now save my wife. At least try."

Two orderlies came over and forced me back out of the room.

I stood at the doors, looking in through the window. The doctors and nurses looked like blue bees, humming around in their hospital gowns. There were so many of them my wife had disappeared behind a wall of people.

I watched as they wheeled the cart with the baby out of the room and down the hall.

I stood at my post peering through the tiny window as they continued to work frantically on my wife. The doctors took turns sneaking peeks at the window to see if I was still watching.

After the ten longest minutes of my life one of the doctors pulled off his mask and gloves.

The others followed suit, making their way for the doors.

"What's happening?" I said as they slowly marched out. "What's going on with my wife? Is she ok?"

They looked from one to another to me. One of them pulled me over to the side.

"I'm sorry, sir, there was nothing we could do."

"What do you mean nothing?" I said standing in his way as he tried to get around me. "Why didn't you shock her sooner?"

"We couldn't risk it with the unborn baby."

"So you used my child to kill my wife?"

"Don't look at it that way. You have a new daughter. You should go be with her."

I grabbed him by the throat and planted him into the wall.

"And you should've asked which one I wanted you to save," I growled in his ear.

"Would you really have told us to kill your child?" he rasped, barely able to breathe.

"To save my wife? Absolutely!"

He looked at me with this strange mix of fear and awe.

I pulled him close.

"You've taken everything from me," I whispered in his ear. "One day I'll do the same for you."

I released my grip and stormed into the room where my wife's bloody body lay still on the table. I took her dangling hand gently in mine and kissed it. Then stared into her eyes one last time.

***

I woke to the exact same beeping. The pitch hadn't changed. This time it was me lying in bed. Everything hurt, not just my hand. And there was no one in the room. The lights were turned down casting shadows around.

I felt as though I was on display in some museum. Light shining only on me, as people came and went with hushed tones.

I had been awake for a while, but never when a nurse tended to me. By the time I roused myself, they had already done whatever they were doing and left. Not having to chit chat or explain why I was here allowed them to do their work more quickly so they could get back to their important job of ignoring patients.

I'd tried several times to open my eyes when I heard someone enter the room, but I was so tired, I never roused myself in time. Then once awake, I would lay there for hours and stare at the walls.

I tried once sitting up enough to look at the rest of my body, but had regretted it. The pain shot my head back to the pillow and what I saw was even more painful.

My body seemed to be wrapped in gauze from head to toe. Attempting to move any appendage resulted in pain. I greatly desired to speak to a nurse at least long enough to find out what happened.

I wracked his brain for hours trying to remember what landed me in this bed, in this condition, but it was useless. At one point I laughably thought maybe my brain was wrapped in gauze as well.

By sheer luck I happened to be awake when one of the nurses came in to do God knows what to me.

I tried to say hello, but what came out sounded like a demon with respiratory problems.

"He... l... l... o," I rasped.

The nurse jolted to a stop and stared at me as if I'd just shot her. She then turned and ran out of the room. A few minutes later she returned with a doctor in tow.

She pointed at my open eye, and said, "See, I told you he was awake."

"Hello there," the doctor said approaching the bed. "How are you feeling today?"

"O... u... c... h... " I rasped.

"I'm sure you're in some pain," he said. "You haven't spoken in a while, perhaps the nurse can get you some water."

She disappeared and reappeared with a cup and straw. They leaned my head forward causing pain to shoot through me and stuck the straw in my mouth. I took a few small sips, each one soothing my throat as the cool water slid down.

"Better?" the doctor said.

I nodded.

"Ok, so let's start again. How are you feeling?"

"I... hurt."

"Understandable after what you've been through."

"What... have... I... been... through?"

The doctor looked from me to the nurse.

"Has he been told anything?" he asked her.

"No, this is the first time he's been conscious since he arrived," she said.

The doctor looked at me and sighed.

"Do you remember anything about the accident?"

"What... accident?"

"Do you remember your name?"

I thought for a long moment and realized I didn't.

I shook my head.

He pulled out a little flashlight and shone it in my eye.

After moving it around he turned it off and sat back, looking thoughtful.

"Do you remember anything?"

I thought about it for a while, then came back to my dream.

"My... wife."

"What about her?"

"She... had... a... baby... "

He sat back.

"Is she here in this hospital?"

"Don't... know... "

"Tracking down the babies that were born in this hospital... "

"She... died... "

"Who died?"

"My... wife... "

"How did you... ?"

"Died... having... baby... " I said, tears pooling in my eye, soaking into the gauze.

"I'm very sorry," the doctor said. "Maybe finding your wife can tell us who you are."

"There would be records... " the nurse said, trying to hide her own moistening eyes.

"Yes, please take a look and see if you can find any births that match these circumstances in the last month," the doctor said.

"Month... ?"

"You've been in a coma for a month."

###

Thank you for reading my story. I hope you were entertained and will return to enjoy some of my other writings.

Please consider posting a review or rating. Reviews are the lifeblood of a book. It's your way of telling the world how much you enjoyed reading it. It also helps me tremendously to let others know what they can expect from this book.

About the author

Michael Kelso is a former Corrections Officer who decided to share his stories with the world. He's been writing for over a decade. Michael lives in Pennsylvania with his wife and family.

To sign up for his newsletter, go here:

https://dashboard.mailerlite.com/forms/399488/88381404106196690/share

Connect with Michael online:

https://mikesimages4.wixsite.com/michaelkelso

https://twitter.com/michaelkelso2

https://www.goodreads.com/author/show/5757505.Michael_Kelso

https://www.facebook.com/mikeswritings

https://www.instagram.com/michaelkelso8294/

https://www.pinterest.com/michaelkelso3/

https://www.reddit.com/user/Horror_writer_1717

https://linktr.ee/authormichaelkelso

Discover other titles by Michael Kelso

Novels

One on One

Identity (A One on one novel)

Endzone

Ties (Book 1)

Novelette

The Mall

Short stories

Dark Tales of Cryptids and Park Rangers

Dark Tales of Cryptids and Truck Drivers

Fragments of Fear

Fragments of Fear 2

Fragments of Fear 3

Fragments of Fear 4

Fragments of Fear 5

Fragments of Fear 6

The Trail

Fragments of Fear: Collection

Made in the USA
Monee, IL
12 June 2023